This book intrigued me so much I could not put it down! This story of a young man's journey into adulthood as he relates to the women in his life, especially his mother and grandmother, was such a great read that had me turning page after page with great anticipation!

--A. Powell

When I first began to read Never Let Go of My Hand I had no idea what to expect. As I begin to read this book I was totally hooked and on the edge of my seat as to what was going to happen next. It was gripping, fascinating and mesmerizing but definitly demonstrates the true talent of Kerry and his ability to bring out raw emotions in his characters.

--G.Graham

Kerry has a way with words that will capture you, and won't let go. Not only was I laughing, but I was crying also. Thinking to myself that Eric was just a shelfish little boy, whom didn't want to share his mama. Getting in trouble all the damn time. Too damn scared to go too his grandma house to spend da night.

-- R. Resse

Men don't like to share their feelings at times. Eric gave me a glimpse of how a young man thinks and feels about his mother. By the time I finish reading this book I had a clear understanding as to why noone can break that bond between a mother and her son.

-- I. Jeudy

There is no surprise to anyone on myspace that I am a loyal friend, supporter and fan of Kerry E. Wagner and loved his book "She Did That". Just so ya know, I loved his next book too. "Never Let Go of My Hand" was more than I expected it to be and the experiences of his character were life changing for me as a reader as well as a mother.

--A. Howenstein

Excellent follow up to "She Did That!" This novel showcases Wagner's uncanny ability to paint a complete picture in the reader's mind while tugging at her heart strings. The characters are very real and remind us of our ever present weaknesses & desires to achieve more in this life. He also drives home the reality that one must live today because there is no promise of a tomorrow. Wagner has a knack for making his audience fall in love with and root for his protagonist who is forever the underdog.

-- C. Elliott

While reading, there were times I would burst into laughter, and there were times I cried. I cried because I'm a mother of one son, I felt the pain. I felt the undying love a mother has for her son. Readers will be touched beyond what is expected, because just when you think everything is going to be alright, something else happens. I feel privileged to have this novel, and look forward to more of Kerry E. Wagner's gift.

-- F. Trotter, author of Thoughts Images & Truth

Never Let Go of My Hand is a modern day African American classic. As I turned each page I was quickly reminded of another modern classic of the black experience, "Manchild in the Promised Land, written by Claude Brown in 1965. Never Let Go of My Hand is written with brutal honesty and a compassion that highlights the bond between a mother and her son...

--A. Collins, author of Untl the Next Time and Until the Next Time 2: God's Plan

When reading this book, I had no idea what I could possibly expect. This book was ultimately a master piece waiting to happen. This book touched my soul in more ways than one. You automatically feel as if you are in the book with Eric.

-- B. Branch

NEVER LET GO OF MY HAND

Also by Kerry E. Wagner

She Did That

NEVER LET GO OF MY HAND

Kerry E. Wagner

www.wagfestlitertainment.com

Edited by Shani Greene-Dowdell, Assuanta Howard, and Felecia Trotter
Cover Design: Julie Hardesty
Text and Composition: Assuanta Howard

ISBN: 09787133-1-1

For information regarding discounts for bulk purchases, please contact Kerry E. Wagner at kerryewagner@hotmail.com.

This book is printed and manufactured in the USA.

DEDICATIONS

Willie & Audrey Crosby, Efrem & Mia Davis, Richard Bolden Sr., Clara Crosby, Carolyn Moses, Shani Greene-Dowdell, Felecia Trotter, Nola Love, Deuce, Boobie, Kiara, Khadeen, Kheranie, Trey, Lewis, Khail, Matthew, Angela Davis, Dena Lewis, Polly, Asha Judda, Anna Rodriguez, Aleshia Abernathy, Julie Hardesty, Bonnie Calloway, Willie D, Reggie Johnson, Harvey Kelly, Assuanta Howard, Jason "Black Magic" Jones, Robin, India Hearn, Trina Harris, Angelica Harris, Trenita Harris, April Howenstein, Amy, The Pratts, The Lodrees, Cathy Dean, Michael Baisden, Fantasia, Tyler Perry, Jay Z, Ice Cube, Keysha Cole, Barack Obama, Sean "Diddy" Combs, Christopher Wallace, Violetta Wallace, Afeni Shakur, and Tupac Shakur.

In Loving Memory

In Memory of my great-great grandmother,
Rebecca "Becca" Alexander, the first woman I
ever fell in love with.

Al Dorothy "Mama Dorothy" Sanders, my dad's
mother – the wisest and most loyal woman I ever
knew.

Ida Marie Bolden, my aunt, the bravest and
most nurturing woman I ever knew.

Bertha "Mama Dear" Connerly, my great
aunt/adopted grandmother – the most unselfish
and most open-hearted woman I ever knew.

Alvin Westley Sanders Sr. & Jr., my granddad
and dad –two cats I never knew, but grew to love
and cherish in spite of.

FORWARD

Nationally known for his controversial blogs and comedic-style commentary, Kerry E. Wagner is spearheading the modern-day revolution of the self-publishing industry. Kerry is firm in his convictions of self-sufficiency, resourcefulness and taking responsibility for your own success, not just in publishing, but in life. After reading *Never Let Go Of My Hand* you will understand why he is firm in these convictions.

In editing *Never Let Go Of My Hand,* I found many tracings of the person I have come to know. No matter how rough around the edges Kerry may be perceived to be, when one cuts through the meat and gets down to the blood that fills the vessels that leads you to the heart that supplies the fillings of his soul you find the truth. Although fiction, the truths released in the pages to follow will at first pull you in with inevitable laughter, but by the book's completion those same words will grip you and perhaps influence you to reflect on where you are in your life. One inevitable question is to come out of this book. "Have I done right by all that have put faith in me and loved me *unconditionally*? Now, without further ado, turn the page and let the powerful words engulf you.

Sincerely,

Shani Greene-Dowdell, African American Literary Award Show Self-Published Author of the Year

NEVER LET GO OF MY

HAND

CHAPTER 1

SON OF THE GODFATHER'S SON

Once Alvin Sanders Jr. was born. Life wasn't gonna be the same for nobody! Alvin was born to give his Mama grief, it seems. But nothing could deter that woman's love for her one and only son. She worshipped the ground he walked on. They say to the point she ruined him rottenly spoiled. Hell, anything he wanted he got basically. From clothes to cars to commissary, if there was anybody he could count on, in his moments of despair; it was his mother... my grandmother. Alvin is my daddy. My grandmother loved my daddy to death.

My grandfather, on the other hand was a totally different subject. He didn't take to being spoiled. He was old school and didn't like anybody doing anything for him. Didn't like anybody doing anything to him either. A big burly red nigga; I always thought of him and his friends as the mob or something. Whenever we went out to eat, my Granddaddy never sat with us or ever sat with his back exposed to the public. He didn't trust anything or anyone behind his back so he kept everything in front of him. He was six feet five inches, two hundred and sixty pounds of red-blooded hillbilly angry Negro man. Hardly ever smiled or spoke to anyone. The most you got out of him above that sinister, mafia whisper, was *"tell Shorty."* The only time he would complete a sentence was when he was cursing out one of his workers.

Oh, "Shorty" by the way, was my adorable, sweet and innocent, but nothing like stupid grandmother. She knew my grandfather was nothing short of an intimidator and they were both proud of it, come to find out. She simply considered the brave ungentlemanlike fella that had arrested her heart and incarcerated it for the rest of their lives... manly.

My grandmother was a very big woman in the church, in the community and in my mind. All four-feet eight inches of her and every ounce of that ninety five-pounded, bowlegged frame. A nice little salt 'n pepper afro she still wears 'til this day, by the way. I never saw her wear any makeup. She had the biggest smile you'd ever wanna see. I got one just like her. That's why the people in my neighborhood called me "Gate Mouf". I didn't mind because it came from my grandmother. I was just proud to be her grandson.

My grandmother never cursed; although, my brother claims to have heard her swear once. But being that no one else ever heard her, it couldn't be documented as truth. And being that my grandmother was the closest person we and anybody else knew to "God," there wasn't no disputing this. Besides my brother was the closest thing I knew to the devil, but not as close as my grandfather, come to find out.

We often would say my grandmother was God. She could look at you without saying a word and you'd hear and feel everything she was saying. She would know if you were lying, before you ever didn't tell the truth. I just never attempted to lie to her...to her face.

My grandfather was considered the exact opposite, the devil. But don't let my grandmother hear you say that. He was "God" to her. The way she spoke so admirably of that man you'd swear he was a saint. My grandfather owned a car lot on the Southside of Dallas. He also owned a club and was talking about opening another club. My grandmother was a homemaker, basically. She worked because she wanted to, not because she had to. Besides her time working, it seemed like she lived in church. That's the only reason I didn't like going over there. Hell, we spent every night in church. Bible study on Monday even though we'd just left BTU (Baptist Training Union) on Sunday night. Not to mention being at church all day Sunday morning and evening. Tuesday through Friday were no different. *Same 'ole thing* as we'd come to say.

Why, because amongst all that godliness, some little devils were bound to form. Wasn't any giving up or giving in where they were concerned. They, being all of us, me, my brother, my daddy, and my grandfather. If my grandmother had her way, all of us would be in church...together.

Known as "The Black Godfather," my grandfather was God down here and out there to our family and in our neighborhood. Kind of a cross between Harry Belafonte and Suge Knight. He was a gambler to my grandmother. Or as she put it, "a man that was going to provide for his family." We simply called him a "hustler." He didn't take no shit and didn't allow any either. My grandfather also had some of the shadiest characters around him known to man.

There was Charles "Boot Leg" Johnson. He never bought anything out of the store. Everything he bought was hot. Then there was Lil' Ervin "Special" Whitfield, the smallest of the group. You couldn't even tell he was grown, but he was one of the most notorious ones. Got the name "Special" because he carried a 38 special revolver. No matter how many niggas was in the gun fight, 38 special was his weapon of choice.

Last but not least, there was "Humphrey." I never knew if that was his first, last, middle or only name. It would be all any of us came to know him as. He was my grandfather's right hand man. I can't ever recall those two saying anything out loud to each other, ever. They were always in close proximity of each other and they always whispered things.

I was familiar with these guys because they followed us everywhere, although grandma wouldn't allow any of them to set foot in her house. When we would go to restaurants, they tagged right along in another car and they, including my grandfather, always sat at another table. My grandfather didn't like to sit with his back exposed. My grandmother didn't seem to mind much that he sat with them, anything to get away from those goons.

I always paid attention to them though. They fascinated me and I wouldn't have minded being one of them. My brother on the other hand, he'd be so busy eating he didn't pay much attention to anything other than what was going in his mouth. He didn't like my grandfather or his friends.

There were a lot more of them, but those were the three always summoned to be with grandfather. They all wore roses or carnations over their hearts on their clothes. They smoked cigars and all talked with a raspy voice, kind of under their breath like. And no one was without a pistol of some sort. I couldn't wait to have one in the small of my back or in my boot. Not to use it, but just to carry it.

My little brother on the other hand, he couldn't wait to pull the trigger. I'm sure my grandmother faced more than enough questions about how and why she ended up with a character such as grandfather. Her answer was simple..."MAN." Which is what she called him by the way ... "Man".

They had one son, Alvin Jr., me and Derrick's daddy. Neither I nor my brother ever knew him, but there was so much talk over him we felt like we did. My daddy was shot and killed when I was five. Actually, I was four when he was shot and five when he died. My dad was what you would call "ruined."

He had and got everything he wanted. He had all the drugs, well syrup is what they were doing back then. He had the money. Not his own, but when he ran out of money, he went to get more from where that came from. My grandmother, she just couldn't stand to tell him no, I guess. And that cost him his life and some of hers too. He was shot in the stomach, and he said they (never saying who "they" were) drove him around and tried to wait for him to bleed to death. Well, let me tell you how I remember it.

My grandmother didn't sleep well at night because both my grandfather and my dad would stay out all night and not come home until wee hours of the morning. So she never slept well because she was concerned if they would actually make it home at all.

Whenever I was over, I slept in the bed with my grandmother. I remember this one night when my grandmother got up to go to the kitchen. Just as she got out of the room, there was a knock at the window. That's all I remember, then somebody whispered, *"Mama let me in!"*

Mind you, I don't even recall ever seeing my father in person, nor have I ever seen a photograph of him with either me or my brother.

4

So this whisper is the only recollection I would have of him alive.

"Mama let me in!"

Wanting to see him so bad, I woke up to tell her. "Mama Dorothy, my daddy say let him in."

She was bewildered by what I told her, being he had a key to let himself in. She simply said, "He did?" I could see the excitement light up in her face that daddy was home.

I assumed after that she thought he would come in the door. However, my grandmother kept it like a mortuary around there with all that fancy ass funeral home furniture, is what I called it. So I was glued to her after that. I wasn't about to go back in that bedroom by my lil' bad four-year-old self. She was gonna come in that room with me, and she did.

On our way down the hall we heard another knock at the side window. It was more like a brushing. You know like a dog trying to alert his owner he wants to come back in the house. Then a faint whisper was there again saying, *"Mama, Mama, let me in."*

Then she replied, "Button?" That's what she called him. "Button, is that you?"

Before he could answer good she was at the front door and I was right there beside her. Though I was scared, I was ecstatic at getting a chance to be able to tell my mama and my brother I saw my daddy for the first time. I wanted to see what he would look like aside from those pictures that were all through and about the house. This was going to be my defining moment.

She opened the door and no one was there. All there was, was a set of taillights speeding off into the night. My grandmother, not sure as to what or who it was for certain, immediately shut the door. She then began to lock every lock in the house. When suddenly the phone rang, it was my Godmother asking if everything was okay with Button. He had just left her house, knocking on the window. When she went to let him in he was gone. This concerned my grandmother now. My grandmother had a remedy for situations such as this...PRAY.

Once she discussed things with God, everything was gon' be alright. My dad often came home in the wee hours of the night, to my grandmother's dismay. So she thought nothing of it. We decided we'd go say some prayers and go on back to bed.

A few hours passed when my grandmother heard a car pull up. Thinking it was my dad; she got right up and went to the door. I stayed in the bed this time. She said, "We're going to surprise him when he comes in and sees you in my bed."

As she opened the door, she saw the same taillights pull away. Not recognizing the type of car it was or with the presence of mind to get the license plate. After the car turned the corner, she heard that faint whisper again. *"Mama, mama...I'm down here."*

She replied, "Button?"

He murmured, *"Here Mama. Down here on the sidewalk".*

Well, my grandmother had a little walkway from the carport that you could see from the street, but from the door where she stood, you couldn't see that part of the sidewalk in which he lay. Shrubbery and bushes camouflaged her view. She stepped outside the door into the mysterious midnight. Took another step down and found her one and only son shot in the stomach murmuring in his own blood. Never making a sound, my grandmother rushed back in the house and got a few towels, helped her son to his feet, and made their way to the car. She laid my daddy in the back seat and came back into the house soaked in his blood. Still without ever saying a word she got me a sheet, placed me in the front seat, and wrapped me up. Without me ever looking into the back seat to get that world famous glimpse of my daddy, I sat my four-year old butt in the front seat curious. I listened to my daddy moan and murmur, *"I'm gon' get 'em, I'm gon' get 'em,"* while my grandmother drove trembling, not to the hospital, but to my aunt's house to drop me off.

What was my grandmother thinking? He was shot not me, but that's how it went down and that's all I remember about that. Six weeks later my daddy died from pneumonia, a secondary condition from the bullet wound in his stomach. He had gone into a coma, but before he went, all he would say to anyone was *"I'm gon' get 'em. I'm gon' get 'em."* He never did.

My grandmother was there January 5, 1971 when he took his last breath. He died holding her hand and she ain't never let go.

CHAPTER 2

DON'T PUT YO' HANDS ON MY BABY!

When my daddy died that day some say some of my immediate family died with him. He was that cherished. My grandfather was relentless in his efforts to seek vengeance on anyone he thought may have had something to do with it. He even went as far as kidnapping and holding some of my dad's closest friend's hostage in undisclosed locations. This was told to me by one of my dad's best friends whom he had tortured that way. He blindfolded them after getting them high off Robitussin, drove them off, and held them at gunpoint, saying if they didn't tell who killed my daddy he would kill them.

Although I heard of granddaddy having a number of men killed, none of my dad's friends ended up amongst them. My great-grandmother and grandfather both passed away also after my dad, six months apart from grief. As was said by my mother, a piece of her died along with my father too. She, for some reason, just always had an undying love for my father. But she had something of his to hold onto and cherish....Me.

My mother never said anything negative about my daddy. Even though I didn't carry his last name because he was off getting high while she was laboring to give birth to my notorious ass. Oh yeah, and she could be quite stubborn. Though she wanted me to be named after him, she chose to use her maiden name and name me after her brother who was constantly making her laugh. His name was Eric and so was mine, Eric Payson.

My grandmother said she actually had him paged at a stadium full of onlookers and witnesses. Supposedly witnessing Prairie View A&M University beat the shit out of Grambling State. Now who would believe that? At least that's what they would claim anyway. But they went to Prairie View, she and my dad. My mother was actually enrolled and going to class when she dropped out to have and take care of me.

My dad on the other hand, he was just up at the school, getting high and driving his so-called no good leeching friends around to different gambling shacks. My mama said to me that my father was a follower. He let his friends use him and she didn't want me to be a follower like that. So she wasn't going to give me everything his mother had. Not that she could anyway. Although she still tried to overcompensate early on, trying to make up for me not having a daddy, by trying to find me one...so hard, I guess.

It started off good, but I wanted my own daddy. All I had was those faint whispers and memories. And I wasn't about to abandon that for no step-daddy. This one step-daddy was different though. My mother had married him and they had a little girl who became my favorite part of having another man in my life to call "daddy." Well it didn't get that good. I just called him by his nickname, "Early". They called him "Early" because of his work ethics. Even at an early age he always had and held a job...and he never was late. So it stuck with him into adulthood, I assume. He didn't seem to mind. He probably was glad 'cause I was one bad little mothaphucka. Excuse me older people reading this, but you know bad when older people would call you that under their breath and between their teeth... just because they saw you coming up the way. You wasn't even close enough to speak or be bad yet. Yeah, I was THAT BAD! Nobody wanted to keep me. Babysitters went home on me, without saying so. Daycare gave my mama her money back, and got restraining orders, and schools kicked my ass out before I could get enrolled good. What kind of way is that for a society to treat a stepchild? So my step dad did what any good _parent_ would've done...put a belt on my ass and that put a strain on his and mama's relationship. Ultimately, that became the demise of that union. See my mama didn't want anybody putting their hands on **her** baby. It hurt her to allow them to do it and once I knew that, **shiiiit!** I played and preyed on that. Shouldn't have ever let me know that.

I would ruin every relationship she thought about getting in after that. Of course, I got a little too over the top with it. After awhile I would pull that dysfunctional ghetto shit at school, and she didn't go for that at all. That made her start whooping my ass. Didn't last long though, she always came back crying about how it hurt her more than it did me. I'd be laughing on the inside.

One time at school, at lunchtime, I stood up on the lunchroom table and pulled my little second grade ding-a-ling out and pissed all over that table and a few lil' second graders in the process. I don't know what made me do it. I must have did it for attention. I got suspended for three days for that. _That's it!_ That's what I was thinking, three days for pissing on your classmates at lunchtime.

My mama felt sorry for me. She blamed it on me needing a father figure in my little retarded life. When that didn't work, she said I needed my father in my life. Well, that was gonna take a miracle. Those few men she did let in told her if they didn't check me, then who? They just wanted to get her to think. And when she never came up with a good answer, they always told her that next would be the police. That statement actually got their asses booted smooth the fuck up out of all our lives. I wasn't sad about it either. Don't be wishing any bad luck on my mama's kids!

Because of the closeness my mother had with my dad, his mother and my mother had a genuine affection for one another. My mother would have me visit my grandmother and I hated it after my daddy was killed. I couldn't stop seeing that casket all over the house. It was bad enough she kept it like a mortuary and my grandfather was never there. Heaven forbid when it was time to go to take a bath, I would never get in that tub alone. Hell, that tub was a casket as far as I was concerned. And my daddy was always in it every time I went in there; at least that's how I saw it. I was getting old enough to sleep by myself, but it seems like right after my daddy's funeral,

I started having issues, like peeing in the bed. I refused to get up and walk down any hallway. They were taking me to all kinds of doctors diagnosing me with this and that. Shit, I knew what the problem was ... Scary! I was scared the dead was gonna get up and get my ass because all during the day, I was "waking the dead" and "raising hell." By night, I was SCARED as hell.

My dad's friend had painted this picture of my dad. I mean it was huge and antique-framed and shit with this sort of halo type glow over his head. My grandmother placed it in the room where my daddy slept, right in front of the bed. Big beautiful heavenly bed too. It looked like if you wasn't dead you was supposed to die in it. My grandmother left it made up the same way my dad left it the day he never came home. Even the hospital gown he wore in the hospital and died in was on a hanger on the back of the door facing the bed along with that big miracle picture staring and scaring me wide awake. So I was glad to be sleeping and pissing on my grandmother at any cost. Until my grandfather showed up at two in the morning and the ammonia attacked his ass before he could get in the room good. Well, that wasn't only my grandmother's bed, even though I don't recall him lying down often. When he did want to lie down he did reserve the right to lie in his own bed.

He told her I was too big to be sleeping with her, let alone pissing all over the got-damn place, and that she was going to make the same mistake with me she made with my dad (as if he hadn't made any himself). Ordinarily my grandmother was boss of the house, but the thought of losing me or my brother, the only connections she had left to her son, all but nullified that. After that, I hated my grandfather too for opening his big mouth. And the one time I was made to sleep in my dad's room alone, I cried so hysterically my grandmother didn't understand. I never acted that way before. When she settled me down to find out what was wrong, I told her the picture was following me everywhere I went. The eyes on that picture would follow me. I would purposely roll to the extreme left or the right of the bed to make sure I was seeing what I was seeing and to make sure I wasn't really retarded. No way those pupils were supposed to be shifting in a picture. I never saw my grandmother get that angry before or after that.

She said, "Boy don't you ever let me hear you say that. ***That's your daddy boy!*** You ain't got nothing to be scared of!"

Yeah, that was easy for her to say, she wasn't eight years old. From that night on, I never wanted to go over there again. Not to spend the night, not to check on her, and not even to call her grandmother. Once I told my mama I didn't have to. Mama always encouraged me to call or visit often though, but I can't remember spending the night after that. I eventually began to miss my grandmother, but I didn't miss that house.

My dad had another son named Derrick. His mother's husband was rumored to have killed my father, but my grandmother didn't want to believe it. However, my grandfather, that was a whole 'nother story. My little brother also had two little brothers that were from his mother and stepfather. So he often came over to my grandmother's house, if for nothing else to get away from his step-dad's drug using, arguing, and beatings.

My mother wasn't the type to be left out of anything though. She didn't have anything against my brother and grew to love him really. She resented the situation he was in once she heard of it. Though she and Barbara got along fine, as far as I knew. I never heard her bad mouth her, but my mama never did things like that to anyone, back bite, backstab, and what not. All my mother knew was Derrick wasn't my grandmother's only grandson. That's why she began to resent me not wanting to go around as much. Hell, she didn't say anything before then.

I guess she feared my grandmother and brother would form some kind of bond that I wouldn't be privy to. But isn't that what grandmothers and grandsons are supposed to do?

Since my mother was trying to overcompensate for me not having a daddy, she figured my grandmother would try to do the same with my brother for not having much of a mother. Because my grandmother wouldn't hear of anyone abandoning their child and beating on them.

Now this one confused me. Here I was needing to get my ass whopped by the good MAN my mother married and she wouldn't let him, and my little brother didn't need an ass whopping at all, but a "nigga" his mother married was beating him all the time, just because he wasn't his. Isn't that backwards, *what's wrong with y'all mama's?*

So he often came to our house too. I used to love that. Everybody did, my grandmother, my mother, even his mother, and especially him. He thought I was a king or something.

We both were very athletic at an early age. I was eight and he was seven. He claimed to be the fastest kid in his neighborhood around his age. Well so was I. I was faster than kids older than me too. Derrick swore when I came to his house one day to pick him up, he knew this kid he admired that could outrun me. I would race against Carl Lewis if he wanted me to, just to prove I was the fastest. So I raced this kid who was about ten and beat him. Not once, not twice, but three times in a row. Each time he wanted to extend the distance we were running to increase his chances. His chances became slim and slimmer.

That day I became my little brother's hero. I cherished the fact he thought so much of me. I would often talk to him about daddy. We both would just dream about having a daddy. Not a daddy, but our daddy. That was special to us. To me, he was my brother; not my stepbrother or my half brother, but my brother. The only connection I had to my father who was that close to me, and we would never let go of that. I wanted to become his protector, just as I was with my little sister.

It was like we had some kind of kindred spirit or angels watching over us. My mama and grandmother would say it was God. Well I had never met him before, so I didn't know for sure, but I could attest to one thing, it was something very different about this blood. At an early age I could feel, sense, and detect it, but I guess hadn't quite connected with it yet. We were definitely gifted with something, or should I say we were blessed with something. Now I just wondered if it was just us like they would say, or was it everyone.

CHAPTER 3

YOU AIN'T MY DADDY

On my ninth birthday my mother was on new husband #2, whom I didn't care for at all. No reason, simply he wasn't my daddy. He wasn't even my sister's daddy, whom I now preferred and wished was around. Had I known my mama was going to remarry again like that, after she said she wouldn't, I would've made it easier for my sister's daddy. At least he moved us into a house. This new nigga moved in with us. For some reason at that very moment, my little nine-year-old mind couldn't figure out what was wrong about it. But I knew something about that was definitely wrong. It was supposed to be the other way around isn't it? The man was supposed to move the family into a home. Not the family and kids moving a nigga in with them. So that perturbed me right away. Besides my mother had done something she rarely had done before. She made a promise and then broke it.

She was driving my sister and I to my grandmother's house for a visit when she suddenly, and out of the blue, asked us how we would feel about her getting married to Frank James (which was his name but who cares?). My sister didn't care; she had her own daddy who would look after her. Who would I have? Not just that, this new nigga was about to steal all my attention and love from my mama. At least that's how I viewed it. Boys have an undying loyalty to their mothers, so I could never say nor do anything to disrupt her happiness if I really thought she wanted it. And she must have really wanted it for her to break her promise to us, because she lived for us. So I acted as though I wasn't fazed by it at all, and pretended to be happy for her, on the inside though my world was crumbling and my little heart was ripped to shreds. Little did I know how fast nor how painful this would turn out to be.

At the wedding, I cried like a lil' nine year old gay bitch. Like someone had died and left me in there with that damn casket all by myself with the doors locked (yeah that bad). Pitiful ain't it?

When my aunt asked me, "Eric what's wrong baby?"

My pitiful ass said "Bay-Bay (which is my little sister) got some doughnuts and I didn't" I didn't give a shit about any doughnuts. This doughnut maybe, meaning this nigga feeding it to my mama in holy matrimony in front of erry'body.

Some doughnuts!! Yeah, that's what they had to celebrate with and the little bity teeny eenie ones at that. Doughnut holes I believe it's called. Something else my lil' nine year old mind knew at that age. One way to know if you gon' marry a nigga mama's...DON'T! If it's on a budget or sponsored by a doughnut shop. The wedding wasn't even a real wedding in a church. It was at one of our relatives' house. Well not actually in the house; outside the house, in the yard. Well not the real yard. Not the good one I mean, the bad one, the backyard. (I know right, a 4th grader wedding hater- shuddup!) As I said, I didn't give a shit about no damn doughnuts. I was furious at the fact that this new nigga had pulled off the impossible. Made my mama betray me and my dead daddy, and there was gonna be a price to pay for that. For him, a hell of a price!

This new nigga came right on in trying to do the exact opposite of what I wanted him to do. After all those years of hearing she needed to let a man put something on my ass, she conceded. Not just any man though, one she would trust around her kids.

What kids? I was *the* kid. My sister went to her dad's on the weekend. I was the only kid left. And this nigga didn't have any so he decided to try to make me his. WRONG!! Very wrong, I was loyal to Alvin Sanders, Jr. Wasn't anybody playing daddy to me. Unless my dead daddy came back alive and we all knew what was going to happen if that actually happened.

This nigga had the nerve to try and make me mind my mama. Tried to help me with my homework, make me eat at the table, and say grace with the family. Aw man, he had life fucked up! *Yeah, I need my ass whooped don't I?*

My mother was even letting this nigga tell me right from wrong. I'm like, "Mama, what you doing? You know the deal! You know we don't let any nigga in between us."

Shit, mama acted like she was on dope or something. And this new nigga was acting like he was her husband or savior. She even got in on the act a little bit.

One day she was fixing breakfast and I assume she could tell Frank James was having a hard time with us, but didn't quite know how to diffuse the situation. Well, once she got through with breakfast she asked me and my sister to take his plate upstairs to him. All that eating at the table and saying grace had been ruined by now. We were now resorting back to our old ghetto ways, and I couldn't have been happier. Until that moment when me and my sister were on the steps arguing about who was going to actually take the plate up the steps to him. My mother overheard us and came to the stairway with an attitude. She said, **"Take ya'll asses up them steps before his breakfast gets cold."**

What! Who in the fuck is "his?" We don't give a shit about his or him. And if you keep this shit up we ain't gonna give a shit about you, Mama! She talking about "his." What about "ours?" Hell, our breakfast was on the table getting cold. She ain't say shit about that. All of this I'm thinking while saying, "Yes ma'am," and walking up the steps at the same time with a humbled look on my face. Because my mama ain't play that smacking your lips and stomping shit. Your ass had to look happy about whatever it was she told your ass you didn't wanna do.

By the time we got to the top of the steps she whispered to us lovingly, "Hey and when ya'll go give it to him say *daddy.*"

Hell no! The tray fell out of my hands and down the steps, eggs, grits, and all onto my mama's face. Then I fell down the steps into and onto the eggs, grits, and all that was on top of her, from disgust. Well not actually, but you know me, that's what I was thinking. My coward but angry ass simply said, *"yes, ma'am."*

He just happened to hear what she whispered to us and when we knocked and entered this mothaphucka was sitting up in the bed smiling with no shirt on showing every bead of his nappy chest hairs. Like we were his kids for real and he couldn't sense the unhappiness in our little stepchild eyes.

Man it took everything I could muster to say "here daddy," and fake smile like he was. Only to look behind me and find my mother right there smiling too, like we're a family and we meant it.

Ain't this a bitch?! I mean literally, my mama is a real bitch right now. Uh-huh, I'm fixing to break this shit up. I'm fixing to start peeing in the bed again...every night, not just on scary nights. Damaging this shit with my destructive ass and making some "U"s in conduct and blame it all on this nigga and her too if she don't chill with that bullshit.(Yea this how lil' boys think and talk when mama's get us a stepdad initially- lol)

He must've sensed I was up to something because he started to kiss my ass a little bit. A little bit wasn't going to do. Not even some major ass kissing was going to help him. Anything short of being my biological daddy was going to be insufficient. But, he was good. He had gotten a better job working construction, along with his nightclub act. He was supposedly a drummer with a band (yeah right). Though I never seen any drums, he wanted to teach me how to play the drums. I didn't want to learn how to play any damn drums. Personally, I don't know if he knew how to play the drums, and I think he was playing my mama.

Football season was coming up and I had wanted to play for a long time, but we didn't have the money before, nor a way to and from practice. Now that I was of age, I wanted to sign up and since Frank James had the money now would be a good time to start calling him daddy. So daddy, he was, all the way up until the time he paid for my registration. Then he became plain 'ole Frank James again. Just in time for me because I wasn't going to be calling his ass "daddy" in front of all those people, but way too soon for my mother. Come to find out this mothaphucka was setting my mama up for the let down. Being all nice and kissing up to her kids and getting them to bring him breakfast in bed while referring to his nothing ass as daddy all the time. Because he was getting ready to break her heart. The nigga ended up leaving my mama for another lady. The reason of choice....ME! Talking about she spoiled me too much. *Man fuck you* were my little nine-year-old sentiments exactly!

My poor mother was devastated though. She felt like a fool because she allowed that fake Sheila E. drum-playing ass nigga to come into our lives and disappear like he was a gigolo and she was a ho. I hated to see my mama crying everyday behind him. It was tormenting me on the inside, until I heard my mama crying to his mother and referring to her as mama.

Mama! What kind of shit was that? That wasn't her mama. It reminded me of how I hated to hear her say that. My sister and

I vowed to never refer to anyone like that, that wasn't our real mother or father. After that, I didn't feel so bad about her crying all the time. I felt she deserved it for betraying us and her own mother. So I just lost myself into football practice afterwards. It was my escape.

One of the other parents would pick me up and drop me off at practice. They were happy to do it because I was scoring every touchdown the team scored. I was a natural and the littlest one on the team. My mother was so depressed and so busy trying to maintain that four bedroom, two and a half bath, two car garage home Frank James promised to help her pay for. She was too tired to come to the games. I didn't notice when she didn't show up, because I had an extended family of my own now. Their names were The Smith's. They loved me and I loved them. I began to stay not just weekends but weekdays over there. Pissing all over their brand new sheets and they never got upset. I was still scared to go to the bathroom. I don't care where I went, all bathtubs reminded me of caskets and they all had bodies in them. Nothing but the devil, I tell you.

My first game was against the Shamrocks. I ran five touchdowns that night. Everybody celebrated me like I was OJ Simpson. I couldn't wait to get home and call my little brother and tell my mother how good of a game I had.

When I got home, who was there fucking up my magical moment? That no-drum playing ass, soon to be ex-husband of hers. She didn't dare look around to see me coming when he was there. I got so bitter I could feel the rebellion swelling up in my little nine-year-old heart. I decided I wasn't going to tell her anything about me. The Smith family was going to be my new family. I didn't even tell her about my game, nor did she ask, not while he was there, or even when he left. Very uncustomary for my mother who always paid undivided attention to me. It was cool, maybe she was tired of me fucking up her relationships. Well her relationship was supposed to be with me, she promised it always would be that way. Promises often got broken it seemed when it came to this nigga. So I found refuge and therapy in the only thing that kept me from losing my spirit, football.

The next game was with the Giants. This game I ran four touchdowns with Eric Payson becoming a household name. The whole organization and league was becoming familiar with my name. I was making a name for myself. Just me, no mama, no daddy, no nothing. Just little 'ole me and something I loved to do. And I was good at it naturally with no training. I now was going to be a pro football player, no doubt. Still with no congratulations, no good game son, no how was your game from my mama, I went to my room and slept with my football and dreamt about how one day the whole world would know who I was. Maybe then she would recognize her son's accomplishments.

The next game we were playing the Cowboys. One of the better teams in the league, but nothing compared to the Steelers who we were playing the following week. I heard so much talk about them, it sounded intimidating.

What was the big fuss? They acted as though I may not score any touchdowns against the Steelers. Touchdowns came so easily for me, but we'd have to get past this week's game against the Cowboys first. No problem, I thought, until after only scoring one touchdown and winning 6-o; that really puzzled me.

I would look over and see the other kids' mothers with their son's jersey numbers on, chanting and cheering them on. I would miss my mama's support the most right then. It made it hard for me to concentrate or focus, it seemed. Not only that it killed my confidence and intimidated me about playing in the following week's game.

Our fans weren't as elated either, because it wasn't as fun No picking me up after the game joisting me on their shoulders chanting "Payson!, Payson!" Nobody was saying "good game" to me. They said "good game" to everybody. I began to feel a little selfish.

Nevertheless, I went home as usual, went to my room and peed all over my bed before morning. This week's practices weren't as fun. The coaches were a lot more serious than usual. I was used to laughing at practices and cutting up because the coaches never said anything to me. This week they were making me pay attention. I was like, *damn, what's up with this, it's suppose to be fun ain't it?* They wanted me to practice for real. I wasn't used to that. I was already good I didn't need practice.

It was the day of the big game, Steelers vs. Mustangs. Eric Payson versus #44 Ronnie Hicks. He was much bigger and blacker than little 'ole me, but I was much faster. This was his second year playing and only my first. They had twice the fans than we had and about eighteen of those fans wore #44 with "Hicks" somebody on the back. Hicks mom, Hicks dad, Hicks step daddy, uncle, aunt, neighbor, whoever. Seems as though everybody was related to Hicks or at least wanted to be. Damn! That was bigger than the game to me and much more than the touchdowns.

The game started and right out the gate, guess who fumbles the kick off return...me, #32 Payson coming to the sideline. I had never seen my coaches look so disgusted in me, like I had lost the game already. No sooner than one of the coaches rolled his eyes at me, the fans jumped to their feet in an uproar. #44 and all his family and friends were celebrating already. Just that quick Ronnie Hicks had ran a thirty five-yard touchdown. Straight up the middle, hurting one of our better tacklers, putting him out for the entire game. The very first play from scrimmage. Hell, I didn't run over him and hurt him. But why was everybody looking at me like I had?

We go back out and took possession. One, two, three, and punt. Three and out, we didn't even manage a first down. I ran the ball all three times with no avail. And who was it to tackle me all three times by himself with no help, but #44 Ronnie Hicks. Talkin' 'bout my mama every time he had done so.

I was thinking "*what's wrong with this little big black ugly kid? My mama ain't even here! Does he know her or something, maybe this was Frank James' baby mama's boy or something.*" Every time he tackled me and I went back to the huddle, and would glance over to that sideline. Seems as though every person on the sidelines and in the stands had despair in their eyes. Depending on me to remove it. That's a lot of pressure for a nine year old, ain't it?

By the second quarter, the Steelers had made three touchdowns. All by Ronnie Hicks. The score was now 20–0 in favor of the almighty Steelers at halftime. I remember thinking, *the Steelers ain't trippin'.* I didn't know if I even wanted to still play running back anymore. The coaches were in an uproar. They were yelling all kinds of obscenities they had no business yelling in front of little kids. In the locker room, I was just off in space. I don't know what I felt. Seems like everything had slowed down and it's a good thing it did because these Steelers were moving too fast, all over the damn place. Especially #44 Ronnie Hicks, but alas we came back for the second half.

We were to receive the ball. I ran out onto the field, standing there chewing what rest of the little mouthpiece I had like it was cotton candy or something. When I saw the Steelers come running out of their locker room, to the roar of all those fans, my eyes stayed glued on #44 Ronnie Hicks and his was on mine. Locked in eye contact with that lil' big black mean ghetto kid, why did he look like a pro football player right then? Suddenly, I heard somebody say "Eric, Eric!" Well, I was used to hearing my name, but this sounded different, but familiar. It sounded like my mama. I looked over to the stands and it was mama.

Mama! Mama! What are you doing at this game is what I was thinking? I couldn't believe that my mama was there. She was waving and pointing at the back of her #32 jersey. It had "**Payson's Mom**" on the back of it.

Oh, no it didn't!

"Hey mama," I waved as I took one last chunk on that mouthpiece. I then rose up a #1 finger indicating I'm fixing to run a touchdown for her right now! She didn't know what that meant; she thought I was just saying "we're #1." She soon found out what it meant as I did just that on the ensuing kickoff. I held up that #1 finger three more times as in touchdown #2, #3, and #4. That's right four second-half touchdowns for my mama. Ronnie Who? Nigga this was Eric Payson fool! If he didn't know before, he knew now.

We eventually went on to win that game 24–20. Ronnie Hicks didn't score another touchdown after my mama showed up. He originally had his whole family there. All it took was my one lil' mama to show up and the game was over.

My mother didn't miss another game after that. She was on the 50-yard line every weekend and that nothing ass husband, well I never saw him again. I didn't care and guess what, after witnessing her son run touchdowns, weekend after weekend, my mama didn't care either. She didn't need him. She had us and we had each other and that's all we needed...sucker!

CHAPTER 4

A WHOLE NEW BALLGAME

I wondered how my mother knew to show up at that game. Well, one of her co-workers whose son was on the varsity team was ranting and raving about the big game that night. She also was ranting and raving about little #32, Eric Payson. I originally was on the junior freshman team for eight and nine year olds, but I was such a natural they moved me up to the freshman team for ten and eleven year olds. The varsity played at night and we played during the day. The lady was telling everybody at work who knew nothing about the league. My mother just happened to overhear her ranting and raving about none other than who, yours truly, her son. Mama was too embarrassed to acknowledge it. She was ashamed because she hadn't even attended a game, let alone participate, so she decided she would come that night. She even invited Frank James. I was so glad that mothaphucka supposedly had those drums to beat on that night, I didn't know what to do. Although he told her he would try to make it later if she wanted to wait. She tried to and when he failed to show. What can I say...he made my day.

Nevertheless, she was late, but she was there on the 50-yard line looking beautiful as ever. Everybody was surprised to see that I even had a mother, seemed like. Everybody treated her so warm and special like they'd known her all along, as if she never missed a game. Making her feel like one of the family. They were a community, a good community of people. Little did any of us know just how important those little league people would become. De-stressing the shit out of our lives for the next four years. Those were some of the best four years, in a row, ever. Undoubtedly they would eventually have to come to an end.

Middle school...now that was a whole different ball game. You had to try out for the team and they were very unorganized. During my little league days the season was pretty long and full of activities. In middle school the season was very short and only consisted of five games per season with too many players to go around. As a result of the short season and me getting bored easily, my grades began to dip. I started getting a lil' musty under the arm because of the hair. We get excited at that age about things like that. I started to form an interest in girls, experiment with drugs, and succumb to some of the peer pressures that go along with being an adolescent. Not to mention coming from a single parent home.

My mother was always at the school and because of that, counselors always made provisions for me. They liked my mother and appreciated the fact that she was a single mother taking days off work to get involved. Now, during this time my mother didn't really have a steady man. I don't even recall one after little league. She was back to dedicating her life to me and what I wanted and I was happy.

Then there was this ninth grade girl at my school. She was taller than I was, but who wasn't, and dark skinned. This was a time when light skinned girls were in, but this chocolate, mocha mint, beauty looked like a black Selena. Her name was Nikki Ramone. She was about five feet eight inches, a hundred and twenty five pounds with long, jet-black, Indian hair, a pleasant smile, and pearly white teeth, just like Selena. She had a small waist, nice round butt, and some baby Beyonce hips, and wore nothing but lip-gloss on her lips. Everybody in the school wanted to look at this girl because there wasn't going to be any touching. All you could do was look. Besides if you didn't have a car you may as well stop looking.

She dated those guys either in high school or just dropping out of it. Fooled around with a few teachers too I heard. (Don't trip, if I was a teacher I would've hit that 15-year-old ass too!) Couple of problems though, none that I would've had to worry about, but she skipped class a lot and smoked weed with the fellas. And she had a bad attitude. That girl was always fighting. Well not fighting because she didn't have a scratch on her pretty little face. She must have been kicking a lot of ass then. But for me to keep liking her, these would be some things she would need to overcome (yeah right). If anything, I would need to become hip. Start accepting, act cool, smoke weed, and act a fool. None of which my single mama was going to go for. So I just liked her from afar. Besides the one time I decided to write her a nice little "you like me" note, it was during the one and only time I would be allowed this close to her. It was in the cafeteria.

I just happened to be eating next to her when she spoke. I got excited and got the nerve to write her a quick note. She didn't even unfold it to read it. She had gotten so many of those little notes that she merely got up and went to another table to eat, looking at me in disgust. I wasn't her favorite student after that. And football playing, she didn't give a two shits about athletes. She liked thugs and thieves. Had to 'cause all the gifts she was getting had to be stolen. I know they weren't able to pay for it. It was too expensive for lunch money, which is all I had. But I still liked her, liked her a lot. Being a seventh grader doesn't garner a lot of ninth grader's attention, so I had issues in the seventh grade when it came to her, lots of 'em.

In the eighth grade, things were looking up. All except one little thing...Nikki had graduated to the high school level. My grades actually started to improve because she was gone. I just could focus better. Plus I was on the varsity team in the eighth grade and I got my jacket that year. You were the shit if you had a letterman's jacket, so I was getting all kinds of action at school now. But Junior high just wasn't the same without Nikki Ramone for me.

Nevertheless, I breezed through middle school without a hitch, most valuable player on the football team my ninth grade year, along with most popular student.

You know I was starting to think my shit really didn't stink now. Had put on a little weight and got a little taller, even a few more hairs on my balls and under my arms. Everybody had hair under their arms before me, it seemed. I couldn't wait to have some more hair under my arms. When I got some more, all I did was wear tank tops or wife beaters. When I didn't have that to wear, I would cut the arm pit out from under the sleeves of my shirts and let the hair poke out...deodorant stuck to it and all. (shuddup!) Actually all it was was peach fuzz, but I thought I was cocky already. Not quite, but I was on my way in more ways than one.

My mother had gotten another job too, finally making some extra money. It was at the airport doing security. She liked everything about the job, except that it was at night. She pondered over taking the position long and hard, but the money was too much to pass on. Considering we were still left with that big ass house and rent to pay, I don't think she ever even considered buying. Anyway how could she? But me and my little sister had a nice place to stay for a change. We didn't have a lot of nice things to wear, though. I mean we had clothes, but not name brand. Our store of choice was a no-name store by the name of Weiner's. A scaled down version of today's Wal-Mart. But the mall for us was as foreign as another country.

Even when we could go there that was what it was equivalent to as far as I was concerned. I wasn't into fashion that much anyway. I was used to wearing hand-me-downs so to speak, which were my cousin's clothes that had gotten too small. Once we began to get new clothes, even though they weren't name brand, I was too excited to know the difference. So it was okay with me, but my mama hated for us to go without or not have some of the things other kids had. It didn't bother us, but I think it made her feel inadequate. So she took this night job and was able to do better by and for us. She was even able to have a little something for herself. She bought herself a car, or as she would put it "us" a car, or as I would put it a brand new car.

Trust me, I eventually found out how brand new it wasn't once it started to break down every other week. That made things really difficult and frustrating for my mama. She couldn't have a man. She couldn't have a career. She couldn't pay her rent comfortably, and now she couldn't have a measly old vehicle. Mama became very depressed and recluse-like. She would just work and come home. The hours at work became longer, so she wasn't cooking as much. She would just take something down and my sister and I would have to fend for ourselves.

As a result of her being so tired all the time she began to teach me how to drive early on because she couldn't see at night. She wanted me to get my driver's license as soon as I turned of age. By now, she began to allow me to take the vehicle out on my own. I was supposed to just run quick errands. You know, like to the store, gas station, or to our aunt's house. But you know me, I never just went where I was supposed to go and came right back. I don't know why, I just never did. My mama would ask what took me so long occasionally, when she wasn't too tired and sleepy. I always came up with some bullshit ass lie. Once she started falling for it and not double checking on me, I sent those lies into overdrive. See my mother totally trusted me. Well now I know it wasn't trust. She believed in me. She believed in the love she instilled in us. It was the same love she had in her. Nothing could come between that, nor did she believe we would ever betray or manipulate that. Well, not deliberately.

Anyway, man I started getting tickets on the car, and would hit damn near any and every pole in a parking lot if there was one. If one wasn't there, I'd find one to back into. It got really bad. That car got so many dents and dings in it. It looked like it had been driven by that crash test dummy. Mama worked at night and couldn't see remember, so she never paid much attention. She even got so comfortable she would let me take the car to school on the days I would be late. Wrong answer! You know I was going to be late a couple of days out of the week now for sure. I was pretty smooth with it up until high school.

In high school I met back up with Nikki Ramone. I had grown up some, but she had grown out. I should've known she was too fine, too early. She gained a little weight, but was still fine. Now she was what we called "thick." Nice, robust, and juicy. However, this was Nikki Ramone and she was still the finest mothaphucka this side of the equator to me. I was still a peon as far as she was concerned, but I had a car and wasn't drinking milk no more. I was drinking Mad Dog 20/20 and so was she, just not with me.

I think she noticed me a little bit when she saw I was driving. The only tenth grader driving like he had his own car. Not just like it was my own car, but like I had paid for it. Anything to gain her attention.

My sophomore year was no different than my seventh grade year. Sophomores gained very little, if any, attention at all from upper classmen. And Nikki didn't pay me any. Those high school dropouts she used to date in middle school were now replaced with grown-up like dropouts.

My grades were failing miserably now that I was driving. I was experimenting with drinking and marijuana more. I went from cutting class during football season to skipping school entirely after football season. Plus I wasn't the star running back anymore. I had gotten bigger and better, but I was still considered small. I was about five feet eight inches, one hundred and sixty pounds, and not only was I not the star running back, but Ronnie Hicks ended up going to the same high school and had gotten a lot bigger.

Remember he was already a year older and a grade higher than I was, so he was a junior now. He was the backup running back on the varsity team last year. Now he was the starting running back. Meanwhile I was a mediocre running back on the JV team, with failing grades at that. In the tenth grade, Ronnie Hicks was six feet tall and weighed one hundred and eighty five pounds. He was now about six feet one and two hundred fifteen pounds and one of the premiere backs in the state. I mean this dude had become chiseled. He looked more like the athletics director than a student. He had passing grades, didn't drink or smoke and was always in the weight room. College scouts were coming to visit him on campus on a daily basis. That caught the attention of who? Nikki Ramone.

I had gotten used to seeing them walking to class, eating lunch, and laughing together. And I would ask myself what the hell would Ronnie Hicks want with her? He got shit going for him and she's a hood rat. Then I would ask myself what the hell do you want with her, Eric? I couldn't answer. Don't know if I even wanted to. But it was the first time I began to think about me, myself, and my status here and in life.

My sophomore year was one of the worst. I ended up failing about three major courses without my mama finding out because I forged her signature on my report cards. I used to forge other people's cards for them too. I got so good at it, I started charging a fee and other students started hunting me down to sign their cards and delinquency slips.

Forging a signature would turn out to be one of my finest moments at Madison High School. Because of my good grown up handwriting, I finally got my chance with the most beautiful, un-lady like female on the entire campus when she needed her mama's signature forged for all of the classes she had skipped. All she did was skip class. That day Nikki Marie Ramone came looking for Eric Jerome Payson to do the honors. Shit you know she could keep that little fifty cents I was charging. She could've convinced me to do everyone's for free if she wanted to.

She skipped so much that we became friends because of it. We'd even skip together and smoke a little weed. Now I smoked, but I never paid for it. Didn't even know how to score it, but she always had the hook up. I was even becoming more popular because of her, but it wasn't the kind of popularity I wanted. Ronnie Hicks had that, but now that running back position wasn't looking so good either.

I ended up in summer school for the entire summer. My mama was very devastated about this. The entire year she thought I was passing, but she never saw a report card, how could she? When I came home on report card day, she didn't know I had my report card. My grades had always been up to par so she never thought to check.

I'd say, "Mama, I got three A's and three B's on my report card."

She'd say, "That's good baby. Now give me my cigarettes off the TV."

That's the only time I didn't mind giving them to her. I hated that she smoked cigarettes. It just didn't look lady like to me. Then why didn't it look un-lady like for Nikki to smoke? And she smoked weed.

We stayed across the street from the neighborhood park and my mother usually looked out her window. Rolling over to one side of her bed near the window where she could watch me and my little sister's every move. When she wanted me to come in and retrieve something, she would simply look out that window and yelled my name. *Eric!* Forgetting she would be looking, I would pout or stomp because I would have to stop doing whatever it was I was doing. She'd catch me pouting and stomping and say, **"stomp your damn feet again and your ass won't ever go outside again!"** I always knew what that meant.

She would have me come awlllll the way inside   from outside. Awlllll the way up those damn steps. Awllll the way down the hall just to say, "gimme my cigarettes off the TV baby."

Man that shit used to drive me crazy. And have the nerve to add on "baby" and I'm a teenager, after she put me on blast in front of the entire park population. I hated that and her for doing it. Funny enough she never called my little sister for things like that. This was the one time, however, I didn't mind giving her those cigarettes on report card day. Because I knew once she put her fish lips around that cigarette for the five minutes it took her to drag, puff, and smoke on, that nothing else was going to matter. She certainly wasn't going to ask for no report card. Now had I gone in there to tell her about my report card and there wasn't any cigarettes I would've had to go get some first.

Anyway, while at summer school at the mostly white Westbury

High School during lunch we would be out romping around. Throwing the football and what not. One of the coaches who was teaching history saw me. He also remembered me from when we played them.

"Are you the Eric Payson that played for the Madison JV Team?" he asked me.

I replied, *"yeah,"* arrogantly with no manners. I was raised to be respectful but I wanted to be "cool."

"How does it feel playing second string when you deserve to be first string?"

I thought to myself, *"What does he mean second string? Why does he think I'm going to be second string?"*

I then replied *"Sir?"*

He said, *"You will be second string because Ronnie Hicks is going to be first string this year and next year. And with you being a much smaller back, you would need more time to impress scouts with your numbers."*

I never thought about it much until then. I was so busy loafing and bullshitting through school, I never thought much about my future.

He said, *"We need a running back here and I know about your grades. You wouldn't have to worry about that here."*

Now he was really talking my language. I told him we lived on the other side of town and wasn't zoned to that school and he said he'd handle that also. **No shit**? That's not what I said, but it's damn sure what I was thinking.

"My mama isn't going to go for that," I told him.

He replied, *"Let me handle your mother, son."*

He took down my information and I don't know what transpired after that, but before the summer was over I had all A's without doing a thing. We moved out of that house my mother worked two jobs to keep and said under no circumstances would she ever give up. The house had been the one thing she had that made her feel like she had something to show for all her hard work. But she did give it up to move into a two-bedroom apartment about three miles from the school...just for me.

In the apartment, my sister and I slept in the bedrooms while mama slept on the sofa. Man the things a mother would do for her son. There is nothing that can come between a mother and her son...I mean **nothing** is what I'm thinking!

(...Yeah right,*" nothing but trouble"*)

CHAPTER 5

SURPRISE, SURPRISE

Well another reason my mama gave into Coach's request, was because they said they would take care of her living expenses. She didn't get anything in writing. My mother was more concerned about my grades, me dropping out of high school, getting into some serious trouble, or ending up like my dead daddy. Which she vowed never to let happen. She always said she wasn't gon' give me everything like my grandmother did him. She didn't recognize that's exactly what she was doing without having anything to give. She in fact was letting me get my way and have my way.

Now the very institution we needed to help conserve and preserve mama's wish would be a major contributor it turned out. The problem was, not to let it get away. The opportunity I mean. We are really gambling here. The whole entire family is riding on me again, little did I know, just as it did when I was nine years old in that game against Ronnie Hicks. But, how could mama bail me out of this. We were officially on the clock and only time would tell.

Well they did everything they said they would. Initially I did all that was asked of me. My mother didn't have to work those two jobs and had time to come see me play. My whole family was coming to be supportive. They were on the 50-yard line every Friday night. With that same #32 on. My mother lived for those Friday nights.

Even though her blood pressure would be sky high at times. She wouldn't miss a game. She started to have these back pains a lot also. The doctor told her to cut back on the soda water. My mama would drink a 32 ounce Coke straight, non-stop, no breathing, no breaks in between until she finished that whole bottle...no bull! Then she would take that kid crying breath that seemed to last about three minutes before you could speak, or before you could die, one.

Well this one Friday night, somebody showed up at my game. They were write ups every week about, me and Ronnie Hicks so there was always some scouts making guest appearances now. My name was being mentioned among the best again.

This fast ass wanna be grown ass young girl, came to my game and my uncle was trying to hit on her. My aunt said that my mama was telling him to leave that young girl alone. But the girl gave my uncle the number anyway. My uncle was borderline wine-o with a major pimp game, though. He had been a very good athlete himself in his day. He was still in decent shape for his drunk ass age. And no matter how drunk he was, he would always come to my games. So I loved him for that. Plus he was funnier than Hell. He kept us laughing; he was as real as Uncle Bernie, as in Bernie Mac and I was his namesake too.   That's how I got my name, remember? He kept my mother laughing all the time. So she named me after him 'cause she was mad at my daddy for not showing up to the hospital. Any how, he tried to holla at any and everybody. He had sisters who were crazy in love with him. He was the baby brother. So he was cherished also just like my dad and me. It was in our nature it seemed to take care of one another. Nothing short of unconditional love was gon' do. Nothing could separate us from one another, except maybe this one thing. This one person. This one girl... who my uncle was trying to talk to, Nikki Ramone. It was Nikki who had given my uncle that number come to find out. Which was cool, 'cause I didn't want her anymore. I started thinking I was too good for her. I had a bunch of white girls just chasing behind me, now. I could have my pick.

But Nikki was giving me the eye that night. I never looked in the stands during a game. The game was on the field, so that's where I'd focused my attention. My mama used to embarrass me all the time, too. She would call my name several times to get my attention. I would hear her and wouldn't turn around. I would put my towel over my head, indicating to her, that I was not going to turn around. She would try to get my uncle to get my attention, anyway. But he wouldn't do it unless, it was halftime. This time there was someone else calling my name. I had heard my name called all my life on a football field, but this was different. This wasn't my mama's voice. This sounded like Nikki's voice and like my mother had done during little league, she finally showed up. It sounded a lot sweeter than I ever heard before, so... I had to see where this music was coming from. 'Cause it was music to my ears. So I looked and on the 50-yard line, right in front of my mama, and there was that chocolate, mocha mint, Selena looking mothaphucka, with that wet 70's lip gloss, sparkling bright, ricocheting off the stadium night lights, like she was my woman, Nikki Ramone. She had gained some more weight, though. She damn near had a beer belly. I didn't give a shit, I was crazy about her. One problem, mama's can always tell when a girl is too fast for you. Nikki was leaning over that rail yelling at me, with about seven other nasty no name, no name brand, hood rats, looking like they were gang members, right in front of my mama. My mama realizing that's the same girl who gave my uncle the number. Even more than that, she realized my so honorable football playing ass, who don't look around at his own got damn mama, looked around for this fast ass lil' pregnant bitch. **PREGNANT!** Yeah, pregnant, 'cause that's what she said after the game.

My mama asked me, "Who was that fast lil' pregnant girl calling you at the game? And I thought you don't look around during games, first off, you little bastard."

"What pregnant girl, Mama? And I don't look around during the game."

"You shol' looked around for that lil' black, fast ass pregnant girl," she said sarcastically.

"That girl not pregnant mama, you..."

As she interrupts, "Well I don't care if she is pregnant. I know who she bet not be pregnant fa'."

"Pregnant, that's Nikki Ramone!" Surprised and bewildered, damn maybe that's why she was gaining weight. All along I thought she was getting fat. Nikki was pregnant, but for who? My mother didn't hesitate to elaborate on her once I told her she was my classmate. She said, "Fast ass, I know why she pregnant too." Then she began to talk shit to my uncle about how he could go to jail for fooling with them young girls. Remembering that it was Nikki who gave my uncle her number. My mother would never let me live that down.

I found out she was pregnant for some grown ass drug dealer about twenty-five years old. She was barely eighteen years old at the time. I remember the dude used to come up to the school after school, him and his posse. In their fancy dope dealing cars, stealing all the girls from us bull shit ass high school kids. I couldn't compete with that dude, football or not. But once the guy found out she was pregnant, he left her ass smooth the phuck alone, that quick. I sort of became the middle man. We began to talk on the phone every night. I even helped her with her baby after it was born. I wasn't doing my chores at home, but I'd be helping her change her baby's diapers. Hell I would barely change my own drawers, imagine that. When my mama asked me to run an errand or something. I would drive all the way cross town. Even if I was supposed to go to the corner store. Getting in trouble for it most of the time. My mama would threaten not to let me use the car.

She got so used to me going to the store, she would be too lazy to go. She'd always give in. Plus I was a king at my new school, now and so was Ronnie Hicks at my old one. The only difference was he was going to class. Me... I didn't attend one single class. I would spend half the day at Nikki's and the other half in the gym—literally. At Nikki's we wouldn't even be having sex. She used to leave me there is the reason I couldn't get back to school on time. She'd be gone in my mother's car. Chasing her baby daddy who was at some other school, knocking up some other teenager with his old ass. I just told my coaches I had a baby girl and didn't want my mama to find out yet. So they fixed it where I could leave school. They didn't care, as long as I showed up to football practice. I got used to it and began to like it. That went on for two years, still Nikki and I never had sex, we just didn't, and I never even thought about it.

(Mmp...I wonder why?)

CHAPTER 6

TIME WILL TELL

My mother's friend lost her job and house. She moved in with us along with her kids. Her name was Belinda and had a son we called Midnight. It was rumored that since he was so dark, his mama wouldn't let him go outside at night. He had a beautiful younger sister by the name of Sundae. She was the splitting image of Ms. Belinda which is what I referred to her as. I was always attracted to Sundae. My mama was praying that I didn't become to emotionally attached to Nikki anyway. *(I say mamas should be more careful of what they pray for.)*

My mother would always try and help people, especially somebody she knew. Ms. Belinda was having spousal problems, along with financial problems, and every other kind of problem. My mama said you never know when you would need some help. We all got along good, though. It was a lil' cramped at first, but we enjoyed the company. Midnight and me would stay up all night laughing and getting high smoking weed. My lil' sister also had somebody to keep her company now with Sundae. That kept her from tattling maybe. Midnight would skip school with me at Nikki' house. We'd both be watching that baby. Well I would and he'd be getting high all day. His mama was mean as hell to him, though. She stayed on his ass about everything. I don't see how he had the nerve to be sneaking to do anything. I don't recall her being mean to Sundae, just Midnight. His mama was finer than a mothaphucka, too. She reminded me of the way Nikki would look when she got in her forties. She was tall about 5 feet 10 inches and 155 Amazon pounds, creamy, caramel, complexion with golden hazel green, eyes, coke bottle physique, with honey blonde, hair at the roots, and the ripest, roundest perfectest titties and nipples ever drew on a bitch, this lady was a **goddess!** Her husband used to beat her all the time, Midnight would say. Which wasn't his real father either. So we had something in common. Neither of us liked or wanted step daddies. His mother was also a recovering addict. Both of 'em drugs and alcohol. She must have not recovered too good. 'Cause she was still smoking and drinking, every time I saw her. But she would never do it around my mother. But her and my uncle was always drinking, driving, joking, and returning from somewhere is all I knew. That probably wasn't the only thing they were doing, 'cause she always had on Daisy Dukes and halter tops with heels, just around the house. I saw her, but didn't really pay attention to her like that. She was Ms. Belinda to me, like an auntie. She always used to compliment me. She'd be saying, "Heey Pay Day, with yo fine self", that's what she called me. 'Cause I was gonna be a pro football player one day and get us all paid. She was real nice. I liked her and the fact that they were there. it took some of the load off mama. She had company at times, even though she'd still be too tired to keep up.

The way Ms. Belinda strutted around that house when my mother wasn't there used to make my day. I stopped going out as much because of that. Just to see her stroll by our room and look in there and wink or something made my mouth water something Niagara, I'm talkin' bout'. Midnight didn't like how his mama dressed, but he dare not say anything. His mama was one mean bitch to him. I didn't understand how she could just be so mean to him and then be so nice to us and Sundae. My mama never did anything like that. I sort of felt sorry for him.

We had the luxury of going in the fridge whenever we wanted to. But they had to get permission. Their mama would be such a bitch, they were terrified to ever ask for anything. As a result of that, my mother put us on rations too. This one day, I had to come straight home to wash clothes for my mama. Since there were more of us in the house, I had to start being more responsible. I had to come home early. Once I got there, I noticed, Ms. Belinda was there also. The blinds were semi-open so I could see, into the living room once I got up the steps. Well I peeked through the window because I saw somebody on the sofa and it looked like they were laying down on their back facing the window. Naw fuck it, she **was** laying down facing the window and it looked like her pants were unbuttoned. Naw fuck it, her pants **was** unbuttoned, but it seemed as though she had her hands in her pants. Naw fuck it! Her hands **was** in her pants, I ain't gon' act like they wasn't no mo. But once I thought I saw that, I snatched my face away from the window real fast. I started panting profusely. I didn't want to startle her and interrupt her itching, 'cause I'm sure that's what it was... itching, right? I didn't know scratching an itch could make a young boy nervous. Obviously when it's done by a grown ass friend of yo' mama's. I decided to stick the key in the lock and jiggle it a bit so that she'd know someone was at the door so she could get herself together. Once I did so, I peeked back into the window blind. She was still in the same position with her hand in those Daisy Dukes. (Okay, it's bad enough they are dukes, c'mon, Ms. B.) I just didn't want to embarrass her. But it seems as though I'm the one who's embarrassed. I'll just open the door and say, "Good evening" and keep going and don't look her way. (Why was I practicing?) ... I opened the door... Why when I opened that door, shut it and turned around, I made direct eye contact with that grown ass lady with her hands in her pants. (**Gyrating**! You were supposed to *not* look dummy!) I hurried up and cut my eyes away, mumbled Good evening and went straight to my room. I took the clothes downstairs, loaded them in the apartment's Washateria, stayed there until they were washed and dried, before I came back up. When I got back after an hour, she was still in the same position. I was hoping she wasn't. (I should've stayed and folded the clothes downstairs, I was thinking.) But I was beginning to think she wanted me to see. But I was still nervous, so I put the clothes down in the living room across from where she lay. I started folding the clothes, holding them high enough to block my view, taking and making nothing more than a glance at her. It started to look like her hand was moving deeper into her Dukes with a slow circling motion. **Oh, my God!** this couldn't be. I tried not to look, but even when I didn't, I could still see her in my head. As I looked around another T-shirt, because the face towels I was folding wasn't doing a good job of camouflaging the expressions I had in my mind. That appeared to be on my face. I heard a zipper unzipping. I couldn't help but take a sneak peek. *Oh my God!* Her hand was now so deep it looked like she only had half a forearm left.

I think drool actually dripped from my mouth at that point. I dropped my head back behind the T-shirt that I ain't never started folding, looked back around it again... Why was this lady looking at me repositioned, sitting up, and back on the sofa facing me, with her legs spread the fuck up and out? Exposing all her neatly placed New Orleans French pubic hair, sliding this exceptionally long finger in and out of her grown pussy hole to my petrified delight. I have you know my heart was having an attack. I laid the T-shirt down, not knowing what to do from experience. But something told me not to move, fast, and don't be in a hurry. With all the other girls I would have went in for the kill, fifteen minutes tops. But this was Ms. Belinda, a Goddess to me. I simply laid back and watched her with my mouth wide the fuck open. My mind doing and going places I never thought it could go. She seemed to enjoy me watching. There was no staring at this stage. I felt like I was traveling somewhere. She was really getting turned on when she pulled the inside of her Daisy Dukes to the side and out slid this wrinkled looking earlobe of some sort. She took her finger and exposed more of it, pulling on it. Her full pussy, vagina, clit, and all were now straddling the center of those Daisy Dukes. It was glistening and moist wit insatiableness. She wanted me see how moist it could get... on my face I think. **What!** I ain't eating no pussy. Nuh- uh, I mean I have not... not before anyway. But unbeknownst to me I found myself crawling across the floor over to this lady.

I ain't even eighteen yet. I don't eat no pussy and why am I crawling? She got me fucked up! I'm gon' stop crawling, right here. I ain't crawling an inch further. My body betrayed my mind as I crawled closer and closer to her.

Meanwhile, Ms. Belinda never uttered a word. She even closed her eyes at some points like I wasn't even there at times. I assumed she was used to masturbating in front of men . I never had before. Well I didn't know I hadn't until this day.

She finally said, "Come here," once I got the nerve to stop. After I swore to myself that I wasn't gon' crawl another inch. I somehow found myself back on my knees baby crawling towards her, again anxiously.

With her taking two fingers and placing her clit in between them, it somehow found its way in between my tongue and mouth. I started off kissing it gently. With a nice and subtle lick here and there, I mixed her juices with a little saliva and darted my tongue in and out of her pussy. With each experimentation of my tongue, she gave me moans of approval suggesting I may have been doing something right.

As she shivered ever now and then, I thought, "*Heeey! I'm beginning to get the hang of it!*"

I raised my head to look up at her and she whispered seductively, "Don't stop baby." She motioned my head with the palm of her hand back towards her clit. My mouth really began to sweat then. I assumed I began to get a little too excited and got a little rough when she lifted my face up with both her hands and told me to stand up. When I did, she asked, "What was that?" referring to that perfectly 11-inch bulge in my wrinkly 11th grade sweat pants.

"Show it to me," she said.

That's when I got really nervous, but I desperately wanted to take it out. I mean it was throbbing something excruciating. So not to ruin the moment, I did as she asked.

I liked the way she was handling me and wanted to do whatever she asked. As I began to unzip my pants, she popped both her breast out. There sat two ripened, ready, thick, nectar-full nipples. They looked so firm, I think milk came out of those titties (shuddup! I'm just saying).

I must have been moving too slow when she said, "No, I want them all the way off, now."

I said, "Right here in the living room with the blinds still open?"

She acted as though the thrill of getting caught excited her even more.

We both began to breathe, pant, and moan heavily. Mine because of nervousness. Hers because of excitement.

Once my sweat pants were down, I stepped out of them. She took my high school dick in her hand and began to massage it firm but gently with nice long rhythmic grown upstrokes.

"Ooooh, awww!" It felt so nice, much nicer than my own hand had ever felt.

She stared at my dick head pulsating at the tip, full of perverted blood like Rudolph the Red Nose Reindeer's nose at the height of Midnight chiming past a Christmas moon.

She put her mouth near it as she stroked it back and forth smoothly, concentrating on the largest vein traveling through it, and the head with the tip of her pointing finger. I was so eager for her to engulf it into her mouth.

When she lay back, wet the tip of her fingers and told me to continue. I hurried up and grabbed my dick and began to yank it something turbo.

When she placed the head of her hand over the head of my dick and said, "No... don't jack it off, baby. I want you to stroke it slooww for me.. I want us to cum together," I was thinking *I don't know 'bout you, but I'm ready to cum right now.*

She laid back, wet her fingertips one more time, closed her eyes, and left me to myself in the center of the living room floor.

By the time she opened her eyes good, I had cum already... three times.

She just smiled and blew me a kiss, and said, "Hurry up and put your clothes on, baby," like nothing ever happened. And you know I really didn't know what happened, but I did know there was a big difference between jacking off and masturbating.

All I knew was somebody else was about to find out too...shol' was!

CHAPTER 7

"DISGUSTINGLY BEAUTIFUL" MS. BELINDA'S VERSION

I've had it hard all my life. My beauty has always been my downfall. You would think something so positive would be an asset, but all it brought me was grief. Oh just in case you thought this was "Eric Pay Day", no hunny. This is the world famous Belinda Pettiway-Boudreaux. It's pronounced (Boo – dro). I say world famous, because if your husband don't know me personally. He definitely fantasizes about me. Don't hate me for being beautiful bitches...I already do.

See I was raped when I was sixteen by my father. He was a heroin addict and my mother died of an overdose of the same poison. My dad actually started out as her pimp. When they both ended up overdosing the state took me and placed me in foster homes, which I bounced around in from the age of six. My grandmother didn't want anything to do with me. She would say I was going to turn out just like my mom and dad. The only reason she planted that seed in my mind was because I was born addicted to heroin and had to go through detox as a baby. So in a nutshell it seems I've been looking for love all my life, but in all the wrong places.

In my search for love all I've managed to find is hate, abuse, and destruction. I hate my situation and that hate has spilled over to my oldest son, Midnight. I don't actually hate him, but every time

I look at him I can't help but feel hate and resentment because he was the product of that rape.

My biological father is his dad. He doesn't know who his real father is. I've always told him that Sundae's father was his dad. Sundae's father name is Ace and had been in our lives since he was two years old so he was all Midnight knew as a father figure. I was with Sundae's father for awhile until he fell in love with me and I had to fall in love with him. It never dawned on me that neither one of us even knew what love truly was. If anything we were in love with the idea of being in love.

Everything was okay at first except for the other ho's. I really didn't have to worry about them because I had a nice car, a huge home, jewelry, and a closet full of designer shoes, clothes, and furs. But after Sundae was born, he seemed to pay more attention to the kids than he did to me. I know it wasn't right, but I started to become extremely jealous of that on the inside. I wanted love all my life, I mean to really and truly have someone love me and he was withholding that from me. I started to resent the fact that I had kids, mainly Midnight.

Ace was shot in the back by another pimp and the shooting left him one leg shorter than the other, walking with a distinct limp. He had to use a cane always after that. That drove Ace crazy and he eventually started using his own heroin himself. In fact I eventually left him over that. It's who I left him for is what is baffling. I left him for Tony, the pimp that shot him in the back. I always had a thing for him. He was soo tall, soo smooth, so calm, and together all the time. Once Ace began to shoot up I became embarrassed for him and myself. It gave me a glimpse of what I may look like. I also began shooting up but without Ace's knowledge about it. He still was unaware when I left him. Sundae's dad wouldn't allow me to shoot up, but Tony did.

After a month's of Tony's constant abuse he was eventually arrested on drug charges. I then went back to Ace, but things weren't the same. Honestly they only got worse and eventually I ended up at Ms. Aubrey's. I think my situation is why she took to me so quickly and I love her for that.

I met Aubrey back in the first grade and even back then I knew she was someone special. She was always helping and encouraging everyone. She wasn't no punk bitch by any stretch of the imagination. She would and could get with yo ass. She was always fighting in school, just not her own battles. She would be defending someone else all the time. Don't let it be one of her kin, no way you was going to win against them. I always used to tell her she was a sucker for an underdog. Who would've ever thought that we would meet up all these years later. I call her Ms. Aubrey out of respect. Even though we are more like sisters, she is more like a mother figure to me actually.

Her ex-husband and Ace knew each other from the streets. Frank James played drums at a local nightclub and Ace used to supply the group with all kinds of drugs. That's the main reason Ms. Aubrey left Frank James. Of course, her being her, she tried to get him help first, but the call of the drugs and nightlife was too much, even for her nurturing soul. She had to do what she had to do for her and her kids. She left him for her kid's sake. I teased her that she left that man for Eric, her son. Her kids don't know the truth about what happened to her marriage with Frank James, which is probably for the best. Her situation gave me the motivation to do right by my own kids. She told me that if I truly wanted to help myself she would help me. After that conversation she told me I could come and stay with her for a little while to get away from Ace.

Not long after I went to stay with her, Ace tried to push his way into Ms. Aubrey's house to see me one evening. He was drunk and high, acting foolish. Ms. Aubrey pulled out her little chrome handled .25 automatic and told him she'd shoot the cowboy shit out of him the next time he tried to pull some shit like that. She told him he had to get himself cleaned up before he could come and see us at that house. After that he never came back, and from what I heard he never got clean. That's when I officially filed for divorce and ended up with Ms. Aubrey and her family a while longer than expected.

After I moved in with Ms. Aubrey, it didn't take long before I'd come to love her children, especially Eric. I'd seen him since he was little. He always was a cutie to me and always mannish even though he thought I didn't know. He was pleasant to me. Ms. Aubrey wouldn't have it any other way, but as he got older, that lil' boy started to become finer and finer. He had the most petite gorgeous physique for a young boy always. But he was putting on weight as a young man. By the time I saw him again he was about seventeen and that's when I made up my mind staying at Ms. Aubrey's was a good move.

The day I moved in that boy came downstairs to get my bags and I swear I think my pussy got wet instantly. He looked like he had a super sized dick and I wanted to see what he was working with. Hell I wanted to touch that thing.

Oh, no, ain't no way, I thought to myself. This was Ms. Aubrey's son, her only son at that. He was damn near my nephew. Besides, his Uncle Man and I had fooled around before unbeknownst to Ms. Aubrey and was extremely good in bed. Child that man could put his tongue in places I didn't even know existed and he was extremely well endowed so I figured that might run in the family.

I had been attracted to men before and gotten hot, but this wasn't a man, this was a boy lighting my fire, not to mention, my best friend's son.

The first couple of weeks were fine because I hardly ever saw him. He was a little football king, which I think was a blessing in disguise. That was until one morning Ms. Aubrey asked me to get them up and ready for school for her because she had an early interview.

That morning, I went into Eric's room and saw something nestled beneath the covers, underneath his boxers that looked like it belonged on an elephant, gurrl! I'm talking about a work of art. I've heard people calling a man's dick pretty, but this wasn't a man. His shit wasn't only pretty, it was pretty goddamn huge! I knew damn well I ain't have no business looking at that lil' boy's dick, but I'd never seen a dick look like that, on soft. I was amazed that he was working with all that and he wasn't even grown yet. I think any woman would've been staring just as much as I was.

I finally turned away sweating, with my grown-woman pussy pulsating. I could actually feel that thing inside my mind...inside me. I decided to cover it up before I woke him. My son was asleep on a pallet on the floor so I woke my son up first and told him to go brush his teeth. When he left the room I tried to wake up Eric, but he was a deep sleeper. For a minute I had to make sure he was breathing. When I realized he wasn't going to wake up, I decided to take one more peek. Hell why not?

I pulled the covers back tentatively and there it was, harder than a rock. I figured it was like that because he hadn't had his morning pee. I know that's what Ace used to say before he'd roll over and stick his dick in me, whether I was wet or not, *Bastard!* His dick had nothing on this boy's though. I was trying to convince myself to let the young boy sleep, but just when I was about to pull the covers back some more, I violated him. I know I was wrong and did much more than cross the line, but I just had to touch it gurrll...just once!

But when I went to touch it, I ended up grabbing the damn thang!! Oh Lord I got this boy's dick in my hands and couldn't let go, took it in both hands too, child. I ain't lying, I did. I wanted to let go, but I had to squeeze it. Damn, his dick was full of blood and throbbin' like oil was pumping through it. I couldn't even squeeze it, it was so much pressure in my hand. (Laughing at herself) I damn near started crying and shouting all at the same time at how good, warm, and thick that thang felt in my hand. When he began to move I jumped, let go and pulled the covers back up over him, quickly half way doing it in the process. I attempted to appear as though I was waking him. I began shaking, chanting, "Pay Day!...Pay Day!" More like cheering huh? Because Ms. Belinda had now become a fan(lol). Finally he opened his eyes and I was gazing down at him gurl. When he woke up I was in La-la land, staring into his sweet and dreamy sleeping eyes. Thankfully he was too disoriented to notice. He did notice that his dick was hard and immediately got embarrassed, so I left out the room as if I hadn't noticed so he could get up. It was amazing to me that he was packing all that to be so young and tender. It was big and he already reminded me of L.L. with his lil' fine self, but I bet L.L. ain't have no dick like that.

I would fantasize and take that situation and climax off what could've happen, but I would always feel guilty afterward. But just like a dope fiend I wanted that lil' boy inside me. Well not him, but his dick. I wanted to see if he knew what he was working with. If he didn't know I was gon' show him. Every time I got the nerve to seduce him, either Ms. Aubrey came home or there were too many kids in the house.

So finally I picked this one day in particular when I knew his mother had something she needed him to do. She asked me to make sure he finished cleaning up before he could take the car. I planned for Sundae and Midnight to go visit their grandmother that Friday and after they were gone I actually prayed and asked the Lord for help. I didn't want to do anything to violate Ms. Aubrey because she had been so good to me, but either the Lord wasn't available or I wasn't listening and decided "what she don't know won't hurt her." Besides Ace always said, cheating was in the game. If you don't get caught, then it ain't cheating.

Anyway, I made up in my mind that I was a grown ass woman and this was my friend's house and I wasn't going to do anything to disrespect her or her house. It would just be wrong, **Dead wrong!** But devilment is in my nature and guess who was coming up the steps? I saw him coming toward the front door. Even though I made up my mind not to do it that didn't mean I couldn't think about doing it. He just happened to come home as I was thinking about it. I couldn't get my hand out of my shorts fast enough so I just left it there. I was dressed provocatively, but I always liked to dress that way. It made me feel sexy and I liked the attention I got from it, it was the only power I had.

I could tell for a moment he seemed to be having a problem with his key. That would've been the perfect time to get myself right, but I saw him peeking in the window like the little pervert I knew he could be and figured this was just too perfect to pass up. I wanted to see his reaction. When he saw me looking he tried to pretend he didn't see me so I was fixin' to fuck with him now.

I unzipped my pants a little more, but tried not to be obvious about it. I wanted to be more suggestive than anything. Let him make up his mind what he wanted to do. A few moments later I heard the door open and close. Even as my nipples began to harden I still had butterflies in my stomach. The whole situation was so silently seductive I just went with it. It had been such a long time since I'd actually been turned on and I was thoroughly enjoying this cat and mouse game.

He came through the door wearing a pair of sweat pants and a tank top. He wasn't that tall, standing only about five feet nine and he couldn't be more than one hundred seventy-five pounds. He was a nice, neat, cut, with broad shoulders, and a thick neck. This young boy was fine, I swear. And the amazing part was he was down to earth, and didn't think of himself as such.

Unfortunately, when he saw what I was doing he bolted toward his room nervously making me very uncomfortable. At that point I was ready to abandon the whole thing. I zipped up my pants but stayed laying on the couch. Next thing I know he was carrying a laundry basket without me having to tell him. And to top it off, he didn't even bother to acknowledge me other than saying, *"Good evening, Ms. Belinda"* when he came in. I was too through after that. At that point I figured I made an ass of myself and was just hoping he didn't have the sense to recognize it or tell anyone.

After about an hour, I heard him coming back up the steps and I got the urge to unzip my pants again and place my hand between my legs and play with my pussy. I figured it couldn't make the situation any worse, so why not?

He came into the living room where I was and sat his fine ass down, dick bouncing around in those Adidas sweat pants looking like he may not have had on any drawers like his nasty ass Uncle Man. He sat down and started folding clothes, holding towels above his face. A smile crept across my face. He knew what I was up to and was now officially a participant in my mind.

When he sat back it looked like he had a whole uncut summer sausage in his pants and it was neatly tucked to one side gurl(lol). The fact he was acting like he ain't see me turned me on even more so I decided to perform for him a little bit. I let my knees fall open, unzipped my pants further, and actually cupped my pussy. I wanted to drive his young ass crazy. I pretended to have my eyes closed and began to rub my clit and moan a little bit. I could see his eyes light up when I did that. He tried to be inconspicuous but he was failing miserably. He stopped folding towels and began folding T-shirts, still trying to hide his face. That was so cute to me. I found myself not only wanting to seduce him, but I wanted to let him off the hook and take care of his little butt. By the time he finished folding a pair of shorts I was sitting up with my legs wide open, and my shorts pulled to the side exposing my entire wet, pink, grown ass pussy to his young ass. It felt so good to do that, *liberating even.* Just to know I was blowing his young mind felt so majestically powerful. I never had this kind of power before, even when I was selling my pussy. I guess it was because I didn't respect tricks. But Eric was innocent. When he peeked around the shirt he was folding I rolled my finger at him looking him dead in the eye, telling him to come here. When I did it, I had no idea the little mothaphucka was gonna crawl, child! (lmao). Yes gurl the lil' mothaphucka crawled (shaking her head). I was feeling like a Queen you hear me.

I took my fingers and spread my pussy and scooted to the edge of the sofa a little. I took my breasts out, stuck my fingers in my mouth and made sure he saw me slide them into my soaking wet pussy.

For a minute I thought he was gon' stop in the middle of the floor, but he kept coming. I mean crawling. I still can't get over that one, that was a damn shame. As he got closer, I started to get turned off a little. Initially I liked the idea of a man crawling to me, but the reality of it set in. He was a boy still and started to look like a little freak, reminding me of those tricks I turned out. It just didn't seem manly, but I still wanted to find out if he knew how to eat pussy since he was there.

Smirking, I knew he didn't after he sucked, smacked, licked

and even tried to drink what little secretions he did manage to produce.

"Stand up," I told him. I thought about sucking his dick thinking maybe that would keep the fire going for me. But that child got up and started jacking his horse dick off so fast that it took everything I had to keep from laughing in his face. I tried to get him to slow down, but po' thang, he just couldn't help himself.

I laid back and thought about busting a nut, but before I could finish thinking about it he was done. I basically just laid there and let him jack off. He was cumming so quick I was fascinated at how he could cum and then get it back up and cum again.

He looked so pitiful cumming too. Whenever I would look at him, I wanted to stop him because I didn't want to waste my time any longer. He was going to take some work and I ain't even have a real job yet.

And I know you probably think I'm trifling, but let me tell you, trifling and disgusting is what makes Ms. Belinda beautiful....Just ask your husbands.

CHAPTER 8

IT HAPPENS

Man! Ms. Belinda was a freak. I was too, I guess. But I was totally infatuated by her. I would want to do anything for that lady now. As if I hadn't already. I couldn't get that lady out of my head. Before now, I only took a shower once, maybe twice a day, but mainly once in the morning. I did that up until I was sixteen because I still peed in the bed. Yeah, a football star and lil' L. L. Cool J look alike still wettin' the bed. Nobody knew but my little sister, though. She would always threaten to reveal it whenever she couldn't get her way. She would have never done that to her Big Bro. To keep my mother from finding out, she would sometimes take the liberty of Febrezing my mattress and turning it over, all by her lil' self, when I was at football practice. We were that close. That's how we were being raised.

Besides my mama would've beaten my lil' sister's ass for having the audacity to tell on her brother, and then beat mine for giving her something to tell on me. My mother couldn't stand for us to tattle on each other, but she demanded we tell the truth whenever one of us was lying. With that, we never knew if we were doing right or wrong.

The only other time I showered was after practice. But since I jacked off on Ms. Belinda I was in the bathroom for hours at a time, just using up whole bottles of lotion and Vaseline. My mother would be knocking on the door saying, **"Eric, get yo' ass out of that bathroom boy!** That water ain't free...bastard!"

She ended everything she said to me with "bastard" when she was upset.

I would have the water just a-running at any rate. I feared that if I didn't leave it running somebody might hear my panting.

When I finally came out, mama would say, "Boy you been in there for damn near an hour. Why yo' ass still smell like the jungle!"

She said I carried a scent because she thought I was bathing and still had an odor. She didn't know I was just in there running the water.

By the time I finished nutting two or three times, I just felt so sleepy that I was too tired to bathe.

On days like that, I would go to Nikki's after first period and just chill over there. She had dropped out of school by then to take care of her baby, but really she wasn't going before then anyway. After spending so much time together, we became really close. Until I decided to confide in her what I experienced with Ms. Belinda.

Got damn, Nikki started tripping like I'd messed around on her or something.

She couldn't stand Ms. Belinda after I told her that. I really think she got jealous or something. She spoke on Ms. Belinda's name something awful. Talking about that lady as if she was any better. In fact, the same things she was saying 'bout Ms. Belinda were the same things they were saying about her in school. That she was a Ho!

I knew it was true, but I didn't care either way...about Nikki or Ms. Belinda. I adored Nikki, and was crazy about what Ms. Belinda did for me. I started to feel a lil' *power* from one female getting jealous over the other; it seemed backwards to me.

I would tease Nikki with the details after that. She was being nosey because she wanted to know and I could tell it was torturing her. She would threaten to tell my mother and that's when I got dead serious. 'Cause knowing about me and Ms. Belinda would destroy my mother. I didn't want to do that to her or their friendship and hell I didn't see any harm or foul in what Ms. Belinda was doing. Nikki claimed it was molestation. *Not if I volunteered,* I thought.

A teacher being some student's fantasy was always talked about at school, and here I was living out mine. I wasn't gon' be deprived of that.

Besides my mother couldn't stand Nikki. She was thewhore as far as my mother was concerned. My mother didn't have a clue as to how much time I was spending with Nikki.

My perception was right though, there was a problem developing. One is the fact that I would always have an infatuation for older women and to be seduced by them. Two, I would develop a need to be needed or wanted by more than one. This created a foundation for becoming an infidel undoubtedly. And three, I was developing an awful habit for becoming very fond of...things and people I shouldn't be. The seeds were being planted, the cancer was growing and the concern was inevitable. But who knew, who could've foreseen what was to come of this.

I simply returned to school and picked up where I left off at home and in my everyday life. I became mannish with my teachers and controlling with females my age, most of all with the ones that were too fast for my liking and just a challenge.

I never liked any of the nice girls that liked me. They had to have gold teeth and dress incredibly provocative *plus* be the World's Biggest Freak. The world was becoming my oyster and I was just in high school.

I got away with everything. Living in an apartment, the athletic department was paying for, getting a free ride with my grades without attending class, and even scouts were asking about me. All the while, I was fucking...well not actually fucking, but fucking around with, my mother's best friend. Having any and every girl at school, not to mention everything I wanted.

I finally got the attention I wanted from the one and only girl who never would give it to me and then it happened. We had to play against my old nemesis and my neighborhood, Westbury vs. Madison. I was determined to show up my old coaches and the shadow that had been lurking over my shoulder my entire football career, Ronnie "Nitetrain" Hicks.

I usually got a lil' nervous before a game, and would have a tendency to vomit before every one. This game I was so pumped that I didn't vomit or take a shit. I was that focused. This was the moment to make or break my lil' career. Senior year in a district game that would determine who would advance to the playoffs. The captain's head out to the field. The energy level is at its highest. This was a classic cross town rivalry. (((((Drums)))) and bands were just playing, so loud you could hear them for miles. Fans cheering and taunting each other, (chanting) **Mar-*lins*!, Mar-*lins*!, Mar-*lins*!**

Tubas played along with them.

For this week's game, we decide to get a lil' ghetto with it. Westbury was a predominantly white school and Madison was an all black school known for its halftime performances from the band, which included a clever number of choreographed dances and guest entertainers.

We weren't known for anything during half-time other than marching – to the likes of *New York-New York* or *When the Saints Go Marching In.* But this week, the band director decided to get jiggy with it. Our band began chanting **"Rebels-In-Tha-House!"** with some heavy bass drums behind it and a two-foot stomp *((stomp-stomp))* twice afterwards.

Man, the Westbury Rebel side went wild! We never did anything extracurricular or spectacular like that before. Even the Madison side rose to their feet doing the Whoosh! Whoosh! Sign. They couldn't believe it.

Well, it would prove and provide to be the boost we needed early because Madison had been kicking our asses since forever. That was until I brought my ghetto ass there and brought a new swagger to the team. It would take a black kid.

We won the toss and decided to receive the ball. Opening kickoff, the kick was high. Usually, that wasn't good because it gave the special team time to cover more ground and ascend upon you. I dropped my eyes down the field for a quick glance and saw a crease developing on the left side. But the ball was still in the air on its way down. I could feel the defense closing in. If I could just hit that crease. I knew it was not going to stay there forever. A few seconds is usually all it's worth, if that much. Just as the ball was coming down into my hands, I accelerated to my left. Just as I did so, it happened. The gap was filled by #57, Greg Jarrett. Just as he filled it, I picked up a block by #31, Ricky Washington. In the nick of time I bounced outside into oncoming defenders, with nowhere to run.

I spun three-sixty around, counter clockwise to my right. There seemed to be a little daylight so I shifted a gear to about three-quarter speed. You never want to be full throttle in traffic, it's hard to change directions that way. I was a natural so it wasn't hard for me. It was instinct.

Just as I accelerated toward the right sideline, this bullshit lil' kicker pops up in my way. I don't know why I didn't run over his lil' Mexican 125-pound ass, but I didn't want to just have a good gain,

I wanted to take this one all the way back. He was nothing, so I gave him a hard step move wide to the right and then suddenly planted off that foot, distributing all my weight from one leg back to the inside left. That kicker was done for. His goose was cooked. I could even hear the crowd go **whoooooh**. Just as I planted, I saw #81, Melton Silas, shooting a rolling block at my waist. Had it been my legs, he would have torn them off. My body went into another three-sixty-degree spin. This time in the opposite direction to my right.

I felt a thud in the small of my back. Not enough to knock me down, but enough to knock me off balance. *Oh-oh*, I knew that was dangerous territory right there in traffic. Unless everyone was holding their blocks. This could be fatal, but with a shifty and cut back runner like myself it would be highly unlikely. As a result of my running style, we led the district in holding penalties.

I was trying to catch my balance with the spin, but spinning and being off balance is double jeopardy on a football field. As I completed the turn or as it was completing me, I saw his eyes. He looked into mine. When I saw his eyes shifting down, mine shifted too. It was like we were in a fight and one realized the other had a gun when the gun dropped out his jacket and hit the floor. Surprised, before we reacted we looked at each other first. Then we looked at the gun on the floor and simultaneously we both made a dash to get it before the other one. Well this wasn't an ordinary moment. This would be a moment to save your life, so it would call for desperate measures. Yeah, this would be one of those moments.

No sooner than I was about to gain my balance, I could see his two hundred twenty-pound frame aiming for my one hundred eighty five-pound knee. This wasn't an average two twenty pounds, no sir. This was two twenty pounds of Ronnie "Nitetrain, nitepain, migraine" Hicks, which he would become known as after that hit. *Pa-Dow!...CRI-CK – CRA - ACKKK!!* OOOOH!... It was heard throughout the stadium(long pause).

....

....

....

....

.....

Complete silence marinated the air. Everyone rose immediately to their feet. My mother and uncle were already on their way to the field.

None of this I knew. The hit was so devastating, it knocked me out, so I just laid there on the field with my body going one way and my leg another, unconscious. My mother and everybody else thought I was paralyzed. I woke up in the emergency triage room in excruciating pain, later to find out my knee had been shattered in five different places.

My first response when I came to was, *"Will I still be able to play football again Doc?"*

The doc replied, "Let's not worry about football right now son."

What? He had life fucked up. For one, I ain't his son so how he gon' just tell me not to worry about football? Did he know that's all I am? Did he know that's all I can be? Or did he know that's how we paid our rent? Did he know they call me "Pay Day" 'cause this was what was going to get us paid? Me and my entire broke ass family. And did this mothaphucka know I ain't seen a classroom in two years? And aside from bullshit, football *is all I fuckin' know !* Undoubtedly not. But worse than that, neither did my mother as she cried hysterically, initially. She had a nice lil' grin on her face when I awoke and asked the doctor that question. She sure as hell didn't have a clue as to what was to come. As the saying goes, 'same thing make you laugh, will make you cry .'

...up in hur, up in hur.

CHAPTER 9

I LOVE YOU TOO, MAMA

I had to have reconstructive knee surgery. After four weeks in the hospital, two surgeries in eight days, and twenty two weeks of grueling rehab, my mama ended up losing her job because she had to take off work so much.

Luckily, the school was still paying the rent and Ms. Belinda and her child support checks were picking up the slack for groceries and miscellaneous items. I wasn't worried. I just wanted to get my knee back right before the next semester when I would be heading off to college. It might not have been division one, but I didn't care as long as I got to one. My coaches and athletic department were very supportive. They even offered my mother a job to start as soon as I was done with rehab. I had tons of flowers, teddy bears, candy, and everyday I was receiving all kinds of stuff.

Come to find out, it was the booster club soliciting on my behalf. It felt like love. And I was, well *we*, were blessed. Seems as though we made a good decision in choosing Westbury because we wouldn't have gotten that type of support from Madison, which was an all-black school in an all-black neighborhood.

The only bad thing about being in the hospital was that Nikki came to see me a lot. With my mother being there all the time off from work, there was no avoiding a meeting of the two. I was glad she was there, but knew my mother would be suspect.

Nikki smoked cigarettes as did my mother, so sometimes they'd meet up downstairs in the smoking area. And neither would say one word to the other. My mother could be stubborn, I told you – and so could Nikki. Nikki wasn't kissing *no* ass, period. She thought she was grown and had a bad attitude anyway. Her eighteen smoking-year-old ass didn't make it any better.

While I was in the hospital going through rehab my mother didn't say much, but I knew once I got out things would change. She wasn't one for biting her tongue.

One night in the hospital while my mother was downstairs smoking a cigarette with Ms. Belinda, Nikki was there and she absolutely refused to smoke in the same place with Ms. Belinda. She took this opportunity to stay up in the room with me. She could be mischievous, at times. Never before with me though.

"I see you got yo' bitch up here. Seventy-year-old bitch at that," she said spitefully. I started laughing.

"That shit ain't funny."

"It's not, but you are."

"Fuck you Eric! You just like the rest of them niggas."

"What? I know you didn't. That's the pot calling the kettle black, ain't it?" I shrugged her off sarcastically.

"That's what I'm talkin' 'bout. You like me, but you hate me on the inside," she hinted about my sly remark.

"You trippin'." "No! You trippin'. You've been staying at my house for a whole year damn near. I walk around in front of you half naked, but you so into that old bitch you act like you're gay." Nikki spat those words out at me like fire.

That's when I went hysterical on her. "Man you trippin'. Ha! Ha! You jealous, for what? I've been at your house and you've been walking around half naked with yo' own clothes off. The baby clothes been off too, you don't see me trying to get on top of her either".

"Why do you like that old bitch anyway?" "What? Who said I like her?" "You don't have to say it. It's obvious mothaphucka!" I bellowed out laughing hysterically and couldn't stop. All of a sudden, in the middle of me laughing, she says out of the blue "pull yo' dick out!"

"Huh?" I said, looking wide-eyed and bushy tailed. That really got my attention.

"You heard me, pull yo' dick out mothaphucka!" she replied.

Damn, that shit turned me on, but I said, "Yeah, whatever."

"Ain't that what that old bitch told you to do and you did it?" Nikki was full of sarcasm this time.

I hated that I told her anything about Ms. Belinda now. I tried to work my way out of the sticky situation, but when she stuck her hand underneath my hospital gown and started squeezing my balls and dick, I was too startled to do or say anything. My mama and Ms. Belinda only went to take a smoke and I knew they had to be through with that cigarette by now.

She lifted my gown up like I had on a dress or something and I felt completely like a bitch. She straddled the end of the bed and began sucking my limp hospital dick right there in that room.

She was surprisingly very good. I mean very got damn good! It could've been just okay, being I wasn't used to getting my dick sucked that much in a hospital room when I wasn't supposed to either. But it was better than good to me. I see how she could catch older cats. She even was looking at me and shit too. I think she was being extra nasty trying to compete with Ms. Belinda. Right as I began to put my hand on the back of her head ***the door flew open!***

Oh shit. I kicked that bitch (and I do mean literally). I kicked Nikki' ass onto the floor with slobber and shit all over her mouth. I snatched the covers up without ever pulling the robe down. Shit was tumbling all over the place. I made complete eye contact with my mama and my dick poking up in a hospital sheet tee pee. Her mouth was wide open.

"*Young lady, I think it's time that you leave,*" she said in a quiet but deadly motherly-like voice.

Nikki got up off the floor slow, not embarrassed at all, got her purse and said "*byyye Eric*" with a sly grin. She mean mugged Ms. Belinda and walked past my mama like she wasn't even there.

I could feel my mama looking at me, but I wouldn't look her way.

71

Finally, she just left the room. Ms. Belinda looked at me, smiled then winked.

What the fuck was she smiling for? I felt like shit, but hell I was seventeen. My mama had to know I was getting some by then. Maybe not.

It's like I knew my mama had two children, but I couldn't imagine her fucking. Me and my sister, well my mama just had us. She didn't have to have sex to get us, ya know? The stork dropped us off. That's just how boys think of their mothers.

The main thing was just not to let yo' mama see your dick...on hard! That would be disgusting! At least, I hoped she didn't. My mama couldn't see that well anyway.

While I sat there feeling half disgusted and half king, when Ms. Belinda came in.

"Your mother is outside in the lobby crying Eric," she said as she eased her hand down on my dick.

She held it, stared into my eyes and said, "I want you to fuck the shit out of that lil' girlfriend of yours for me, for looking at me like I ain't a queen bitch, okay? Then after you do, I want you to come get on top of me and tell me about it til' I cum, you understand?"

I nodded and she walked back out of the room.

That was too much. What was I gon' do? A few minutes later my mother came back in and went through her same routine she had every night. Washing up, getting ready for the next day of rehab. She plopped down on the couch beside my bed, said her prayers and when she was done all she said was, *"Eric Jerome Payson! Don't let me catch that lil' Hussy 'round here or my house again. You understand me?"* Before I could answer good she said, *"I don't give a damn if you understand or not. If I do, both of y'all asses gon' be down on the flo' with slobber on yo mouf next time. I betcha that! Now good night...and I love you!"*

"Good night mama. I love you too." I said, snickering in disbelief to myself. How could I not love her for that? How could I not love everything about her...ain't no way.

...This was my mama.

CHAPTER 10

YOU DON'T MESS OVER MY BABY!

No more crutches after today. Didn't matter much, between Nikki and my mother, I got the royal treatment. Mama was at the hospital everyday and the Nikki fucked the shit out of me daily. I hadn't gotten around to Ms. Belinda yet because I was cooped up in the hospital.

On the way home, my mother was acting kind of strange and vague. I couldn't make her behavior out. Then it hit me, they are going to surprise me with a welcome home party. I just knew it, but I wouldn't dare ruin it for her.

Yep, that's what it was. My welcome home gig. The whole complex was there and it turned into one big block party. Nikki was there, and by now we are all up under each other. My mama hated that. Nikki on the other hand was loving every minute of it. Not loving me. She was loving the fact that my mama was so perturbed by her ever living presence up under her son. Mama used to talk about her so much it seemed to make me like her more. I felt as though mama wasn't giving her a fair chance, but she gave Ms. Belinda a chance. To me Ms. Belinda was the bigger ho. But I liked ho's obviously.

The party was lovely. It was great getting to see family and friends again. But the shit really hit the fan when it was time to go back to school and my coaches tried to get me to entertain the thought of going back to class. I was like, 'Go to what class? I don't even know where I'm supposed to be.'

One coach replied, "Algebra."

Algebra! I ain't even been to regular math yet, I thought, feeling the air slowly leaving my lungs. They were taking the life out of me with this class shit.

Then my head coach told me I couldn't leave the campus again during school hours, either.

What!? I was sure I was dying then.

I don't know which one I was more disappointed in, having to go to class or not being able to see Nikki during the day. She wasn't allowed at my house, so our time together would be cut down drastically.

Man, by the time I did go to one of those classes, they treated me like a stranger. It's like the whole class knew my status. Football season was over. Not just that, come to find out my football season was over—forever.

The school called my mother regarding my grades and she came up to the school. When they summoned me to the office, I wasn't in my class. I wasn't even on the campus. My black ass was where they told me not to be. I was at Nikki' fucking all the pussy she had left. Like it wasn't gon' be any left tomorrow.

My mother, on the other hand, was given a laundry list of classes I failed, tardies, and absentees I had while I was there. She was humiliated. When I got home at four o'clock, strolling in like I was cool and had been at school all day, I was met with a barrage of kitchen utensils, all in succession of one another.

First, a skillet went whizzing past me. Then I ducked a spatula. A canned good skimmed the top of my head. *Oh, shit!*

Then a heel of some sort came flying towards me. It must've been Ms. Belinda's because my mama didn't wear high heels. Anyway, I bobbed that one too. I had to weave it too 'cause it seemed to do a boomerang of sorts, as it missed me and came back without her throwing it again. *Whew!* My mama did all of that while calling me everything but a child of God.

"Mama! Mama! What I do?"

"Mothaphucka! Oh, you think I'm stupid, huh?" My mother was angrier than a raging bull.

"Huh?"

"You think I ain't ya mama, huh? Mothaphucka!" she screamed while looking for something else to throw at me.

"It was an accident mama," I squealed. All of the seventeen-year-old deep leaving my voice. I thought she might have been upset about the dings and dents I was putting in that old car.

"Wait a minute! You think I'm something to play with, don't you, you bastard! It ain't no accident." She hurled another item at me. "That yo' ass wasn't at school today. That's why I'm 'bout to accident-ly kick yo' ass."

"Oh, shit!" I thought out loud.

"Yeah, 'oh shit' is right mothaphucka!"

Mama was going to have to settle down for me to tell her the whole story. I bailed to my room getting hit in the ass with a few objects I can't even name along the way. I shut the door and pressed up against it and wouldn't let her in. She was like a lady possessed banging and beating on the door. There was no way I was gon' open that door. I tried to explain.

"Mama, just let me talk to you, pa-lease."

I could hear her breathing heavily, and could tell she was settling a bit. I had to be careful because my mama could be crafty as well. Act as though she wasn't mad, then commence to tearing yo' ass up.

"My coaches knew I wasn't going to class, ma. They are the ones that gave me permission to skip classes. How do you think I was passing if I wasn't going to class? Since they are not able to use me anymore, they don't want to have anything to do with me. That's why they are changing on me, mama."

She wouldn't believe me. She kept ranting about how good that school has been to me and the kind of opportunity it provided.

I said, *"Mama, they have been changing my grades the whole time."*

She still wasn't buying any of it. She said we'd go to the school tomorrow, and if she found out I was lying, *"I ain't never known an ass whoppin' like the one I was gon' get."*

Well, I didn't know about any of that. *I ain't catching no mo' ass whoppins, I'm tellin' ya that,* is what I was thinking. Mama had life fucked up.

She was furious the rest of the day. I did everything I could to avoid her. There was no such thing on a day like this. I was a slave until midnight, cleaning everything from the rooter to the tooter. I noticed Ms. Belinda 'nem hadn't come home or even been there that day. I didn't think nothing of it.

The next day, mama and I were on our way to school. I was nervous all the way there. We get to the principal's office and the principal calls the coaches to the office to defend the allegations of the grade changing. I should have known something was up because the principal already knew. She didn't need to call the coaches.

Man, these folks had their shit together. They even told my mother I had a baby and they only allowed me to leave at lunch to tend to my baby. *Oh! Snap!* I didn't want my mother to find out about that. That was a good one.

My mother wouldn't let go of that one. She swore up and down she knew there was a reason I was under that lil' girl so much. To my surprise, she was even more disgusted I wasn't claiming the baby. She wouldn't let me get a word in edgewise.

Do you know the coaches and faculty had the most despicable grins on their cheesy ass faces. As my mother apologizedand the looks on their facesleft me feeling used, a fire lit in me that was going to be hard to blow out. I'm sure they could tell I wanted to kill them right then.

I couldn't hear my mama either with her shit, for believing them. I didn't even try to dignify the baby accusation with an answer. I never acted like that with her before, but we were at school. There wasn't gon' be no embarrassing me at school...no mo'.

On our way back to the bus, one of the assistant coaches who was one of the few black coaches there, knew my mother, pulled her to the side and sprinkled some of the truth on mama. He also said, he told Belinda about it several weeks prior.

The assistant coach, and the only one with some integrity said, "I don't know why she didn't inform you."

This Bitch. This Bitch was fucking my assistant coach too. That's why he and my mother were so cool. So it's on now.

We couldn't wait to get home. My mother couldn't wait to see Ms. Belinda, and I couldn't wait to ask her about this coach.

When we got home Ms. Belinda, Midnight, and Sundae and all of their shit was packed and gone. Ms. Belinda had left the fucking building. Yeah, just like that.

Then we found a letter on the table from the school.

Due to the status of student "name and such" not being in standing with the school pre-requisites and requirements we have the misfortune of informing you that he has been dropped for the semester.

All this had been done a month prior while I was in the hospital. The mothaphuckas even had the nerve to charge me for the books I didn't return. The worst part was they were no longer going to take care of our expenses, which meant no rent, and my mother was still without work. The good thing was they still had a position for my mother. She just didn't know when she would be starting. That part, they never told her.

Meanwhile, we were in the process of finding out how many summer school classes I had to take, and how much make-up work it would require for me to graduate.

With the help of the assistant coach, we also found out that the athletic department had been turning away college coaches who came to inquire about me. That's why I never met any college coaches. I was being blackballed. The book on me was I was lazy, uncoachable with a bad attitude, bad behavior, and failing grades.

Not to mention every time my mother inquired about her new position, they gave her the runaround. Eventually, she realized the same thing was done to her. They used us. Once her son had no more to offer. No more touchdowns to run. No more stadiums to fill. No more coaches piggybacking off her son to move to the next level of coaching. No more tickets to sell out or news articles to write about Eric Jerome Payson. The game was over, but they had fucked over the wrong ones in the game.

"You don't mess over my baby! You can mess over me, but you don't mess over my baby." That's what my mama would come to say. We tried going to the school board to expose them. We tried the NAACP. We tried writing the newspaper and news stations. Well, not we, but I found out my mother was doing all of this to no avail.

My mother got even more intense about it when Nikki told her the baby wasn't mine. It didn't help much when she told her the real daddy was a grown ass man, damn near thirty. Mama wasn't feeling that, a man abandoning his seed. That man had better stay away from mama.

CHAPTER 11

GET THE HELL OUT

My poor mama was tired. We eventually had to move into a smaller apartment, two bedrooms, when there were three of us. My mother had found a job cooking and doing dishes at a small nightclub restaurant.

I completely dropped out of school, but mama refused to allow me to just sit home during the day for fear I might get in trouble or end up making babies with Nikki. She would make me go to work with her. Shit, I decided I'd rather go back to school after that. She was working me like I was a Hebrew slave, on purpose, I think. She didn't like the fact I was so comfortable being out of school.

Listening to her nag and fuck with me all day didn't make it better. She was getting on my nerves so much until I didn't give a shit if I went back to school or not. I just wanted to get away from her.

The final straw came when she started bartending at night for the same restaurant/nightclub. She would be there all day and then all night.

Eventually, mama was able to buy a used car from my grandfather. Around that time, she also started dating this guy that used to come into the club. His name was Skipper Lee Johnson, an ex-boxer turned car salesman.

He was aight, I guess. I didn't mind him because he kept mama occupied, and she didn't act so angry when he was around. That's the only reason I liked him. Besides I could use the car whenever he was around. Before then, mama had completely stopped letting me use it because I dropped out of school.

Well, while mama was out buying the car from my grandfather, she introduced Skip to him. Skip told him he was the used car manager at a local dealership. He and my grandfather made arrangements to do a couple of deals, being my grandfather was a wholesaler himself.

It was one week after my mother got her vehicle when I went on a ride in it with Uncle Man. Skip was over so ya' know mama didn't mind that we were gone in her car, I guess so they could get their groove on. Kool Cup, one of my friends, was over and he tagged along without telling his mother. We were supposed to be bending a few corners and that's it. We ended up at this *tittie bar/gambling shack/rib hut/auto detail shop*. It was a hole in the wall for sure. It smelled of whiskey combined with pussy, cigarettes, and chitterlings. It didn't make any sense to breathe in there, but we did.

We took a seat right in the front. Well, if my daddy's side of the family was the stand-up side, my mama's was the opposite. All drunks with bad attitudes except for the girls. The girls had the bad attitudes also, minus the drunkenness. Uncle Man was the ring leader of the Wine- O's, he was drunk before we got there. He was all in the place showing off for us, like we ain't never seen pussy before. I'd seen enough pussy to know not to touch none of the skeezers sliding up and down those rusty ass poles.

It was bad enough we weren't old enough to be in there anyway. They acted as though they didn't even know ID existed when we came through the door. The waitress was old as my grandmother's, grandmother's...grandmother and her boss was twice as old as she was. I don't know if his hair was gray or it was full of spider webs. He sat back deep in the corner by the door at the entrance. Wasn't nobody leaving without paying is what I took it to mean.

Uncle Man was loud and boisterous, pointing, talking about

everybody, and pouring us drinks we don't even want to drink, until we were drunk as he was. I felt sick and didn't care how drunk I was. I wasn't drunk enough to be doing what he and Kool Cup were doing to them nasty, played out strippers. That was until guess who comes out sliding her sexy ass up and down and around one of the rusty poles? Yep, none other than the ruler of my dreams, fantasy of my imagination, love of my life, none other than the one and the only, (((((drum roll please))))) Yours truly... Ms. Belinda!

That bitch bailed out on my mama and betrayed both of us. Fucking my uncle and the assistant coach at the same time and now, she was sliding her rusty pole riding pussy I forgot and never got to fuck all over me, my uncle, and my friend. Uncle Man had been coming to see her, all the time knowing where she was. I was hurt and really ready to go now.

She started working her magic on me and got overly aggressive, making Uncle Man either very furious or very jealous, maybe both. Then he got overly aggressive with her, pulling her close and smacking her on her tail feather. None of which sat well with the antique gentleman behind the bar that owned that fake ass, bootleg, burlesque, barbershop.

He looked old and slow but moved mighty quick. Next thing I knew, he had Uncle Man by the wrist with a cane in one hand and a shotgun on the shoulder of the other arm.

Uncle Man tried to snatch his arm loose, but that old man must've had a hell-u-va grip, 'cause he didn't even budge. It embarrassed the shit out of my uncle for me to witness this. What did he do that for?

Uncle Man folded that old man up like a lawn chair and that's when that old ass waitress came out with a cute lil' derringer.

Shit, me and Kool Cup were already at the door, but my uncle was still cursing and talking shit, "shoot me then! I ain't scared to die."

Yeah, he wasn't, but we sure were.

Uncle man was actually taking his time exiting the place.

The old man was punch drunk and dizzy still trying to collect himself as his wife, the antique waitress, helped him up. By the time he did get to his feet, my uncle was about to enter the car, talking shit like he was Muhammad Ali. Talking about how he 'shook up the world.' '

"I shook up the world, I shook up the world!" he screamed.

All of a sudden the old man appeared around the corner of where we parked and yelled, "she might didn't shoot yo' ass, but I will, God damn it!" He started pumping that twelve gauge.

Boom! Boom! Boom! – Boom! Boom! Boom!

Six shots went off from a twelve gauge. I didn't know a twelve gauge could reel off six rounds, but it was a twelve gauge with a clip. We all hurried into mama's new car. My uncle had already gotten the car in reverse by then.

Backing up, I could still see fire spewing from the barrel of the old man's gun. I even saw the scowl on his face. He meant to kill us. Too ignorant to duck, or too scared, one, I sat straight up in the car not knowing who was hit. We burnt rubber backwards through and out of the parking lot.

"Everybody aight?" My uncle asked drunkenly. We checked ourselves to see if we had any leaks. I looked in the backseat to see if Kool Cup was dead or alive, 'cause he didn't answer, he was not even in the car.

"Oh, shit Unc! Where Kool Cup at?!"

"I don't know, but if Kool Aid ain't in here he got to find his way home 'cause we ain't going back to get his ass."

Oh, that's another thing my uncle would do, completely fuck up your name.

"Kool Cup Uncle Man, it's Kool Cup, not Kool Aid Unc.'"

My uncle paid me nor Kool Cup any mind, keeping his pedal to the medal heading home.

"Noooo! Uncle, we can't leave him."

As we approached a red light, my uncle said, "I'll make the block for his ass, if he ain't there, that old ass nigga back there don' prolly drained his Kool Aid."

"Okay, okay!" I said, praying silently that we ran across him. We made the block, but no Kool Cup.

Then I heard a faint calling from a distance, much like the one I heard when I was four years old; the last time I heard my daddy alive.

Then it got closer..."*hey...Hey...HEY!!!*"

"There he is Uncle!" Kool Cup was running up behind the car, so I reached back to open the back door.

Refusing to stop, my uncle kept driving at a slow pace until he caught up. Kool Cup ran track, so he caught up in no time. He was scared as all outdoors.

We sped off running every red light we encountered. By the time we got a few blocks from the house, the car would not accelerate over ten miles per hour so we ended up coasting home. We parked and went upstairs like nothing happened. Mama and Skip were still asleep.

The next morning when my mother was getting ready for work, she went downstairs to warm up the car. She never did that before, but she was so proud about having a car she was trying to take care of it by warming it up.

Suddenly, she came back upstairs with that stern Clint Eastwood look on her face, and said, "Eric, where did y'all go in my car?"

Afraid to answer, I said, "To Uncle Man's friend's place." I made sure not to say friend's house, just in case she knew the truth already.

She said, "What friend?"

"I don't know his name."

She replied, "*Come here.*"

We both went downstairs to the car. The car was still running... knocking... clucking... clicking... clanking...and knocking, with steam and smoke coming from six different holes in the radiator. That old man shot that damn car up.

Mama slammed her fist down on the car and it almost fell apart from the force as she screamed, "If you don't tell me what the fuck happened to my damn car!"

I knew better, so before she could finish good I started tattling like a bitch, telling her everything. Before I could finish sangin' on his ass, she was already on her way up the steps to wake up Uncle Man.

It was over, her cup had runneth over. She had her fill. That was the last straw. That was the day I never thought would happen. My mother was tired of us, and mainly me, messing up everything for her. We had destroyed her brand new car, a week after she purchased it.

"Get the fuck out...NOW...both of you!" I don't give a shit where you go, but you got to get the hell out of here...TODAY!"

...*And don't come back! As she slammed the door.* (((door slam))))

CHAPTER 12

TO START OFF FRESH

"Nikki what time is it?"

"Twelve thirty a.m. What? Boy, yo' mama ain't worried about yo' ass."

Nikki stayed with her grandma and I was locked up over there all night after my mama put me and my uncle out. I never saw mama that mad at me and didn't think she was serious. She usually would have given in by now. But maybe she didn't know where to find me. That's when the phone rang. It was Midnight, Ms. Belinda's son.

He said, *"Eric, me and mama gonna' come get you. My mama say you can stay over here for awhile."*

I didn't have anywhere else to go that I knew of and couldn't stay with Nikki', so I said, "Okay, when are y'all coming?"

"Give us forty-five minutes," he said.

I didn't want to tell Nikki, so I told her my mama had Midnight to call. Being he was the only one who knew how to get in touch with me. Forty-five minutes was just enough time for me to hop on top of Nikki. I knew she wouldn't turn me down now. I think we fucked the whole forty-five minutes straight for the first time. Shit, that was a record for me.

Midnight and his mama came and picked me up. No sooner than

Midnight and Sundae were asleep, Ms. Belinda came into the room. She had on a beautiful, white, sheer, satin negligee, with a robe to match, and heels with fur on them or something. She stood in the hallway with one hand on the wall to the right above her head and the other on her hip. I just sat there in a still-like awe, fascinated by her beauty. I'd never seen anyone that beautiful before, that close up.

"You just gonna lay there?" she asked with a nice purrr to her voice.

I hurried to my feet to meet her. She turned and grabbed my hand and proceeded to her bedroom.

I felt light, like I was walking on air. Just because she grabbed my hand and held it. She was holding my hand and that just felt right from her to me. It felt like she wanted me and not just to seduce me.

Naw, that can't be. She's a thirty-seven year old grown ass, sophisticated woman and I'm only a half assed eighteen-year-old dropout with nowhere to stay, I thought.

She shut the door and proceeded to the bathroom and ran some bath water. I still was standing at the foot of the bed. I was ready!

When she returned I was told to get undressed and hurried and did so like I had on a one piece. As I stood there naked, one candle was being lit, then two, three, and so on...all over the bedroom.

She turned on some nice jazz music again grabbing me by the hand with a nice pleasant smile as she led me into the bathroom. This bathroom was plush and very feminine. She told me to get in the tub and *whoo!* The water was extra hot, but I didn't want to act pussy like, so I dealt with it. I thought she was gonna get in with me, but she knelt down with this hard wash glove and began lathering it up.

She said, "You should always make sure your body is extra fresh whenever you are getting ready to make love to a woman. You do want to make love to me, don't you?"

I nodded yes.

"Well, I have to teach you how to do that and you can't make love to a woman funky, just wouldn't work," she laughed and added, "but I'm sure you're having enough sex."

She paused and looked at me suspiciously. "I could smell it on you when you got in the car, nasty."

Oh snap! I hadn't washed off after I got off Nikki. I was getting ready to look embarrassed when she took the sponge, dipped it in the water and placed it on my forehead, as she "squeeeezed" all the water and bubbles out of it onto my forehead.

Niiice...that's how it felt, nice. Then, she lathered it up again and asked me, "What part of your body do you wash first?"

"My chest," I replied feeling like I was in heaven.

"You always wash your face first, nasty. You don't want to clean your ass and then use the same towel to clean your face," she said as she washed my face, talking to me and complimenting my features as she did so.

Mmp, I never thought of it like that, but it did make sense to wash your face before your ass. Here all this time I had been wiping my ass onto my face (shuddup! You prolly do it too) She then lathered up and washed my chest and back thoroughly. I almost fell asleep from the back washing.

She asked, "Have you ever had someone bathe you before?"

"Uh-uh," I responded.

"Stand up for me young daddy."

Oh shit, she called me young daddy and I almost fainted from the rush of feeling like I was one...without a job. As I stood up, she got off her knees, slipped her heels off, raised the robe up and sat on the edge of the tub placing her feet inside the water. Opening her legs a bit, she pulled up her robe around the lower portion of her hips. I began to get excited and she moaned and suggested, "Mmp-mmmp. Not yet., You are going to learn to take your time tonight." Lathering up the sponge glove again, she began washing my shoulders, chest, stomach, ass, legs, and feet. "Saving the best for last," she added rolling her long lashes and eyes toward my genitals.

She took the gloves off and lathered her hands up and placed her hand on my dick, she then pulled the skin back, since I was uncircumcised and squeezed the head of my dick, only.

"Did you know that this carries bacteria?" she asked.

"Nope." I damn near whimpered when she asked me the question as her hand eased gently over the head of my dick, again.

"You always have to make sure you pull the skin back before you pee too, okay?"

"Okay," I replied, submissively.

"Promise me that," she said, steadily working her soft hands from the shaft to the head of my uncircumcised dick.

"And make sure you dry it real good too," were her last words before sanking the mushroom part of my dick into her mouth, with the soap still on it.

"Mmmmm...see that's better, not so salty."

She looked up at me with soap still on her lip gloss and said, "How do you feel... young daddy?"

I didn't know what to say, so I just closed my eyes and went back to heaven.

"Isn't this nice?" she asked.

"Better than nice," I responded.

"That's because I am making love to you right now," she murmured with that twinkle in her eyes and on her lips that I will remember for a lifetime.

Man, this was better than sex already!

She rinsed me off, dried me up, lotioned me down, and then licked my entire body clean as I lay on my back. Taking her tongue from the inside of my toes to the inside of my thighs, along the inside of my balls, up and around my shaft, over my dick head, dipping in my navel, a dab or two, tightening her teeth a bit on both my nipples, up one side of my neck, lapping my chin and ending in my mouth. (WHEEEW!)

She then neatly slithered up onto my throbbing rock of manliness taking her time as she magically took me off into a euphoric bliss.

I had my eyes closed the entire time and so did she. Only peeking a bit when her body would start to herk-n-jerk and shiver-n-quiver. It was then that she tightened and tried to catch her breath before releasing an insatiable sigh. Uhhh.

Niiiice, again! She was getting one after another, after another, after another. Each time telling me not to cum yet.

My entire back ached by now. She rolled over half out of it and while catching her breath said,

"You can cum now, baby. I'm sorry."

I started to try for it, but she was asleep before I could finish. I simply got a cloth and wiped her gently with it, got up, blew out the candles one by one, turned off the radio, pulled the blanket up over her naked body and went back to the living room and fell asleep without ever busting my nut. I was just okay that she was *okay*.

I'm not sure if that was *making* love or not, but I'm sure it *made* love. *Made* me fall in love with Ms. Belinda's ass. I didn't want to go home after that. I was over there about two or three days without even calling home. I was gon' show my mama I didn't need her and I could make it on my own. Ms. Belinda wasn't making it any better fucking and making the shit out of some love to me every night. Not to mention, just down talking my mama like they never were best friends. Saying how mama was controlling, over protective, and insecure. She even had the nerve to say that my mama loved every man she was with.

'That's why you are rebelling, Eric. I understand.'

Given the fact that my mama was so stubborn and hard to communicate with, I thought, *yeah-yeah, shol' is. She the one that let me take the car. I don't even have a license.*

Ms. Belinda then sealed the deal by claiming my mama just needed some space so she could be with Skip, insinuating I might be a problem. Since I had been a problem thus far, well that was devastating to think of and would be my excuse to do as I pleased.

I got so jealous I called my mama just to piss her off and tell her where I was and that me and Ms. Belinda were having an affair. But, I ended up only telling her where I was. She got pissed off still, and demanded I come home. I asked her if was she still involved with Skip.

She said, "Yes, he has moved in and I'm not asking him to leave because he is helping us!"

I immediately declined to return saying, "He ain't helping me. I ain't ask him for no help."

She adamantly replied, "Well you can stay where you at until you ready to come home and start being responsible. I am still your mother and this is still your home." Before she hung up the phone she ended our conversation with, "I love you," and paused for effect.

I just hung up the phone without saying it back, despising Skip's ass completely now.

Come to find out, some kind of way Ms. Belinda and mama had a conversation. I doubt very seriously it was a conversation, but Ms. Belinda got upset with me for telling mama I was at her house. It's like I ruined her plans or something. She really was trying to spite my mama. That was the first inclination I got that Ms. Belinda may very well be jealous of my mama. She also got paranoid I would tell mama what had been going on between us.

I tried to tell her I would never do that, but it was too late. She had already agreed with mama that she wouldn't allow me to stay there, so I had to leave. I still refused to go home. I felt like I couldn't after I spoke so adamantly about not going back there. I was gon' show her.

After mama and I argued back-n-forth about it, we agreed the only place I could go was my grandmother's house. Not my dad's mama, 'cause I still didn't like staying over there at all, and hadn't for about thirteen years. I just visited occasionally. Besides, my lil' brother was staying with her now permanently. I did think about it initially, but her hands full with him already.

I knew if I went to my dad's mama's house, I would have to go to school and be responsible. If I went to my mama's mother's house that would be more like a vacation. Nobody but the girls finished school up there, and that's just where I wanted to be. My mama's mother didn't know how to say no, so of course she asked, "What yo' mama say boyee?" when I asked her could I move in with her.

"Mama said, it's okay. My mama even bought me a bus ticket." My mama initially told me I couldn't take nothing I didn't pay for myself and if I wanted to be a man 'we gon' start right now, but as usual she gave in.

I had one more night to stay home before I left Saturday morning and couldn't wait. I got up to go get a blanket and ironically my mother and Skip were both gone leaving only me and my lil' sister in the house. Just as I set up under the cover, I heard a loud noise. **KA-BOOM!!** I jumped up. Then I heard another **Ka-Boom!**

I was afraid to move, but it sounded like someone was trying to break in the apartment, so I rushed to the bedroom where my sister was and made her get up under the bed. For some reason, I got in the bed she was in. I pulled the cover up over me allowing the side not facing the wall to drape down over the side of the bed so my sister wouldn't be noticed.

"Stay down there and don't breathe if ya' can help it," I told her, quivering over each word.

After the third Ka-Boom the front door kicked in and some raspy voiced old man said, "Eric. Eric!" It sounded like my grandfather, but what would he be doing here? Again, the voice called out "Eriicc!" as it traveled down the hallway.

I reluctantly said, "Hah?"

Coming directly to the room where he heard my voice, he responded happily, "Hey boy! It's just your granddaddy."

I sat up surprised and elated. He sat on the bed next to me,"Where is Skipper and ya mama?"

"I don't know, but let me get my sister."

"Naw, that's alright. Everything alright."

I said, "No, she right here, under the bed."

Granddaddy and I scooted over to let her out. Placing her on his lap, he laughed and gave her a peck on the forehead.

"What you doing under there?"

"I thought somebody was breaking in." I answered for her. "I was gon' let them kill me, but not my lil' sister."

Expressing his delight, he reached out to give me one of the finest of handshakes. I noticed a man standing in the door and it was Humphrey. "Hey Uncle Humphrey."

With a serious look on his face, he said, "Hey Champ."

My grandfather nodded his head for some reason and then asked, *"Say, what time ya mama be home?"*

By the time I could tell my granddaddy I didn't know, I heard another **Ka-Boom!** My mother's bedroom door was being kicked in by two other men. Both toting shotguns.

My grandfather, without breaking a sweat with the same demeanor said, "They gon' look around a lil' bit. So, how many touchdowns you run this year?"

He attempted to keep me distracted, but I said "seventeen" without ever looking at him. My eyes were glued to the gentleman carousing about the house– Bootlegs, Humphrey, and Lil' Special, which meant somebody was in trouble. I was hoping it was Skip, and it was.

Granddaddy didn't say what for. He simply said, "Tell ya mama and Skipper ya granddaddy came by" and handed me and my lil' sis a crisp one hundred dollar bill a piece. It looked as if it was fresh off the press.

I surely needed the money since I was leaving the next day. Amongst all the ha-lay, I forgot to tell granddaddy about me moving. Me and my sister didn't go back to sleep after that. We stayed up and watched TV until mama came home.

When mama and Skip came in, they saw things were not the same. My mother immediately suspected I was trying to fuck something up for her, so she went off on me.

"That's why I'm glad yo' ass getting out of here! That's all you do is fuck up shit. I'm sick of you! I mean it!"

I politely let her finish before I told her what actually happened. She was seething.

Skip had the look as if a terrorist was after his ass. Mama called grandmother (my dad's mama) to tell her, but remember I told you grandmother was "nothing like innocent." My grandmother adamantly denied it, knowing all along it was my grandfather. To appease mama, she claimed to have asked him about it and he said no. Knowing my grandmother, she probably didn't ask him. She simply told him about it. They were a perfect cunning pair and I wanted me a woman just like that.

My mother was furious at them both! She never would have thought my grandmother would lie to her, but she didn't believe what she said, not one bit.

Skip hadn't paid off his debt with my grandfather and my grandfather came to collect. (Know what I mean?)

Me, hell I was satisfied. *That's who she was putting me out for? That nigga,* I thought to myself.

Later that day, I was on a bus ride to Mississippi to start off fresh. I know everybody was looking for me to fail, but I would show 'em. I wrote Nikki a letter since I didn't get to see her before leaving; I was too wrapped up in Ms. Belinda1 bout couldn't remember to breathe. But I'm headed up yonder way now. Jackson, Mississippi, make way for Eric Jerome Payson 'cause here I come!

CHAPTER 13

THE RAWEST OF THEM ALL

My mama's family was dirt poor. Eight to nine people to a house, every house. I was about to be number nine or ten at somebody's house. But I always had fun up there because we were always laughing and cutting up.

The only problem was nobody went to school. My mama's daddy was a small-time Baptist preacher, plus an alcoholic, and a fighter. I mean he'd be beating up deacons and shit at his own church. My grandmother was the most prissiest, beautiful lady you'd ever want to see. She loved being catered to. She basically didn't have to do anything for herself, drive or nothing. She never had a job, except for having ten girls and finally four boys – that was her job, raising those fourteen children.

I had numerous cousins down there, too. All of whom loved to fight – each other, I mean. But they all loved me. I never had any problems with any of 'em.

As soon as I got there, I met a grandfather I never met before. Oh yeah, I'd seen him, but this was a different grandfather than who I was used to seeing at Thanksgiving or Christmas when we visited. He immediately began to hit me with the rules. The law of the land was you had to pay your own way, meaning you had to work, which meant you had to get a job.

Damn. No wonder nobody was in school. They had to drop out to help take care of "everybody."

Literally, everybody took care of everybody. Not in a good sense. There were just too many for my grandfather to take care of and he didn't believe in women working. So none of them did. Either they had a husband to take care of them, or their brothers, uncles, and daddies did.

I wasn't trying to work, but after a couple days of not eating like I was used to, I found my ass at McDonalds working the night shift. I also quickly found out that I didn't want to live like that, so I enrolled back in school. I was gonna try and surprise myself and get my diploma.

They had gangs in Mississippi, which I didn't respect 'cause I was from a big ass city, Dallas. Those fake, country ass wanna be's trying to have gangs was hilarious. They were called the "Raw Dawgs." They all had numbers on the back of their shirts, Raw Dawg #1, Raw Dawg #2...so on and so forth – all the way up to #65. They were a joke to me. I'd be damned if I got to wear a number, it ain't gon' be nothing other than #1.

However, Raw Dawg #3 and I became really cool. He was in my gym class. I used to tear his ass up on the basketball court, so we got cool. He was the only one I was cool with though. He used to invite me to wherever they were gathering at. I was bold and cocky 'cause I was from the big city, so I didn't bar those hillbilly ass niggas in Mississippi. They wanted to get at me, but Ray Ray, which was Raw Dawg #3's name used to make my bond. I guess since I came with him, I was his responsibility. I didn't give a shit though. I had my own chip on my shoulder.

They didn't let it ride easily though. They stared and watched me like a hawk. Even at school, it seems like I crossed every Raw Dawg at some part of the day. When I really lost respect was when I heard how Raw Dawg #1 talked to Raw Dawg #2 like they weren't even potnas.

It finally came to a head when we were walking to the park one Sunday. Me and two of my older cousins, Barry Bee and Benny Gee. Both of them were twenty one and stayed high. Some real ass thugs, always in trouble with the law. We were all walking down the sidewalk and here comes two of the Raw Dawgs, #1 and #9. They were both walking down the same side of the sidewalk as I was, #9 behind #1, of course.

I could see the look on his face as we came toward each other, like he'd been looking for an angle to get at me and this was his chance. I was sort of behind my cousins a couple of paces. They were up ahead smoking and scheming about something, I'm sure, and not really paying attention. It never registered until afterwards that they sidestepped my cousins giving them the right away, which meant respect, but they probably didn't know I was with them because I was so far behind them.

As we got up on each other, I didn't move nor did Raw Dawg #1. He wasn't that much bigger than I was, about six feet two, a hundred ninety five pounds and a few war wounds on his face. The other was about five feet nine, a hundred fifty five with a bunch of war bruises all over his body. Raw Dawg #1 got as close as you could allow a person to get without hugging and that's when I pushed him off. Expecting it, he automatically got into his fighting stance. He had baited me in.

I'd been waiting for this moment and so had he, apparently. The moment for me to show him I didn't give a shit about a Raw Dawg – I'm **my own** Raw Dawg!

And he was ready to show me, "You must not know who we are. We are the RAW DAWGS! and I'm Raw Dawg #1, the rawest of them all." (engage!)

We are in an all out war before my cousins came to the rescue. Initially, they didn't break it up because I was getting the best of him. Until he began trying to wrestle instead of fight. Ain't no wrestling where I'm from. That's surrendering or an indication you are dizzy or tired. When #9 pulled out his knife, both of my cousins pulled out guns. "Make me leak yo bitch ass nigga!" Barry Bee yelled.

Benny Gee who loved a good shoot out playfully suggested, "I wanna shoot this one, he don't look like he suppose to be alive anyway," pointing his gun at the weakest ones head.

I got mad and told my cousins, "Naw mane, let me have this Ho!"

Bennie Gee reiterated, "Nawl, y'all can fight, but I'm gon' shoot this bitch with his punk-ass knife."

Barry Bee alerted, "That's my lil' cousin, **HO!**"

They both looked startled to hear him say that. Immediately, they began to plea with them saying, "Say Barry Bee, we didn't know man."

Meanwhile, I got insulted they were taking up for me like that. I don't need nobody taking up for me; that was humiliating, but there was no negotiating at that point.

They knew my cousins from around the way and didn't want any part of them. I was mad and insisted I would be a laughing stock because I had to go to school with those fools and they didn't. They thought I was overreacting. When I did go back to school it was exactly the opposite. Ray-Ray (Raw Dawg #3) came up to me laughing hard as hell.

He said, "Maann why don't you join our gang?"

I declined as I'd always done and he said, "Man, I told them you were real! They got much respect for you now. Not because your cousins are Barry Bee and "Benny Gee, but because you didn't tell anybody that they were."

"Tell somebody for what?"

"Dawg, Yo' cousins put in work." Work meaning doing dirt, so they are respected."

The Raw Dawgs were extra friendly and ever courteous after that. I still wasn't impressed, but I didn't have any problems with them nonetheless.

I still could not avoid trouble it seemed. One day, I was at work at McDonald's joking with this cute chubby girl. I didn't have a girlfriend because I couldn't get used to how the females looked up there. Let's just say, compared to the females in Dallas they weren't the most attractive people to me. But this one was cute, she was just tipping the scale a bit. I knew she had a crush on me, and thought she was friendly until her boyfriend showed up and actually jumped the counter.

He came back into the grill area where I was flippin' Big Mac patties and asked ferociously, "Who is Eric?"

Before answering, I made sure to get a grip on the grill cleaner next to the grill.

"Who wants to know?" I said matching the intensity in his voice.

"Kickstand!" he replied proudly.

Kickstand, I repeated, puzzled. "I suggest you start using the name yo' mama gave you, but I'm Eric, so what's up?"

"Meet me outside nigga!" he said as he turned away quickly.

This nigga was crazy for real, but oh well. I stopped working and went around the counter not knowing what he had on him or his intentions. I stole on him before he got out the door good. **BLA-DOW!** He went straight to the floor screaming like a bitch. I started stomping him until my managers pulled me off him. He hurried up and burned out of that parking lot.

Because we didn't know if he'd come back with a gun or something, my managers let me leave early. They decided it was best not to jeopardize any of the other employees.

The next day at work, everybody was bragging on how I kicked "Kickstand's" ass. He was supposed to be this bad ass everyone was intimidated by. Even his girlfriend was laughing claiming she was tired of his "jealous ass." She just so happen to not have been at work the day before.

Yea, right! I personally think she provoked him deliberately. However, I wasn't feeling her too much after that. I didn't appreciate her jeopardizing me like that, so it wasn't that funny to me.

Later on during my shift, while I was mopping the dining area when guess who pops up? None other than the notorious bitch, *Kickstand.* That fool could have shot me or something. I thought he was coming back to pick up where we left off, like I would've done. So Instead of waiting for him to make a move or say something, I grabbed the mop handle and initiated a confrontation.

"You want some mo' nigga?"

Stunned, but brave, he took the position. Although valiant, he fell short again as I kicked the shit out of his no-fighting-but-brave ass...again. He will learn to lean on his kickstand next time to keep me from steadily knocking him over on his ass. He limped back out of the restaurant and his girlfriend went outside to check on him.

Come to find out, I kicked the shit out of a borderline handicapped niggas' ass twice. That's why they called him Kickstand. He had one leg shorter than the other and wore that funny ass boot. Hell, I didn't think to look at the size of a nigga's shoe if he talked shit to me. I thought he thought he was cool or something.

The sad thing was that he didn't come to fight that time. He had only come to ride the bus home with his girlfriend. Hell, I didn't know! You can never be too careful, slip up and that's your ass Mr. Postman, ya know, with these wanna be ass gangstaz.

My managers put me on probation for the second fight and I was officially making a name for myself in Jackson, Mississippi. I was becoming known as a troublemaker. The word got back to my grandmother and she was concerned. She didn't want my mother to think I was up there running wild.

Speaking of mama, every time I talked to her she kept saying, *"You gon' see. Ain't nothing like being at your own house."*

All I could think of when she said that was "why Skip ain't at his then?"

105

It had only been two weeks since I left home and I'd already been in three fights and got chased home in the middle of the night a couple of times for mouthing off at a couple of Hispanic gang members driving pass.

Seems like I used to get chased home all the time. They'd say something and I'd shoot the finger, grab my dick, and taunt them after they drove past a distance. Like clockwork, they made a U-turn to get my ass. I sought cover running through this cemetery at night, and I do not like dead people! I would tell my grandfather hoping he would come pick me up at night.

He said, *"I suggest you either quit mouthin' off or find you a new route home."* So I did. Only to find out that he would in fact come and get me...on payday! He was always there on payday, so I never had any money left. And the funny part is I never told him when payday was. He just was good with calculating and keeping up with every man in the house's pay date. I wanted to go home so bad now, but I dare say so.

I missed my mama.

CHAPTER 14

IT'S IN MY BLOOD

One day before I went to work, I was across the street visiting one of my friends I went to school with. We were chopping it up and catching up on what's been going on at school when my cousin with one glass eye came across the street to join us. Before my grandfather left, he told him to cut the grass. If you don't know anything about down south, those are some big ass yards.

Instead of him cutting the grass, he gonna come over and bully me into cutting it. *Don't he know I been kickin' ass lately?* Plus it was about thirty minutes before time for my bus to come.

He knocked on the door, abruptly, like he lived there. Then, I heard my homeboy saying, *"Eric. Yo' uncle wants you."*

He wasn't my uncle, but he was that much more older than me, so everybody thought he was, even him.

I came to the door, and he said, "Say boy, daddy say come cut this grass!"

I already knew my grandfather told him to do it, so I said, "He didn't say me. He said for *you* to do it."

"Nigga, I don't live there," my cousin screamed at me, about the grass he was supposed to be cutting.

I told him "well, go tell Daddy that" knowing he would never think of doing that. My grandfather didn't play that, much like my mama.

That's one of the reasons my mama and her oldest sister moved to Dallas. They didn't like nobody telling them what to do. (Sounded like somebody I knew.)

My cousin replied, "Oh nigga! You think I'm playing. Let me have to come back 'cross here."

He went back across the street thinking he had me scared. I just went back into the living room with my homeboy, laughing. 'Cause I knew he was furious he had to cut that grass, and he was not man enough to tell my grandfather no.

I looked out the window and saw he was having the most difficult time getting that lawn mower to rev up. This only made matters worse in his mind, I'm sure. Not only that, he looked up in disgust and desperation from his attempts at starting that lawn mower. He saw me and my friend looking out the window. With him being my kinfolk, and having one eye, he may have seen the snickers on our faces as well. He wasn't happy about that at all.

No sooner than my grandfather got into his old beat up truck to leave and pulled out of the driveway good, my cousin was on his way marching back across the street. By this time, we were sitting on the porch watching him. I sat out there purposely because if my granddaddy wanted me to cut the yard he would have seen me when he pulled out of the yard and told me so. But he didn't. He just waved and kept on going.

Furiously, my uncle-cousin stormed up the steps. I had that sly grin on my face that he didn't like. "Nigga! You better come help me cut this grass." It went from me *cutting* the yard to me *helping* him now.

Ordinarily, I wouldn't mind, but it was fifteen minutes before I had to catch my bus so I told him, "Man, I'm fixin' to go to work!"

"Man?!" he said, "Oh, I'm Man now?"

"Duh..." I said sarcastically, "Naw, you ain't, 'cause if you was you wouldn't have been scared to tell Daddy you don't want to cut that grass 'cause you don't live there."

What did I say that for? Nobody! I mean _nobody_ in my family likes for anyone to think that they are scared of anybody.

He didn't even respond...the next thing I knew was – WHOP! Right in the mouf, not the mouth...but mouf. Hitting someone in the mouth down south was when their mouth was closed. Hitting them in the mouf was mid sentence and caught errybody by surprise .

I fell to the floor.

"Who you calling scary, nigga?"

I said "scared" not scary, daaang, I thought.

Damn, I didn't have time to respond. Shocked, I just grabbed my mouth and looked at him in awe. He was already on his way back across the street as if he just knew I was following behind him.

Oh, yea, I was followin' his ass alright, but it wasn't to cut no grass. It was to cut some ass. I calmly hopped down off the stoop, walked across the street, went into the house and quietly changed from my work boots into my tennis shoes. I was careful not to disturb my grandmother who lay sleeping on the sofa close to the window. She could always be found there.

I went back outside, up the driveway thinking he may be on the other side of the house cutting the yard, when I should have known better from the audience we had already front and center across the street. Out of the blue, this fool leaps off the porch like he's Spider Man.

I jumped, but it wasn't quick enough. His old ass was throwing a punch in mid air...and caught me good with his flying sucker punch.

Oh shit!

I recovered like it was nothing, I was used to fighting.

Bing! Bing! Bing! Three crisp jabs as I stung his ass with that D-town three piece, and when it looked like that glass eye was halfway out the socket – **BAM!** I knocked it all the way out. He tried to wrestle me after that, but I told you ain't no wrestling where we from. I slammed him up against the house and he fell onto the ground.

I could hear my grandmother screaming out, "Buster Lee!"

Buster Lee was his name, by the way, which was ironic because he was always getting into fights, but it was his face that always ended up "busted" up. That's how he lost his eye the first time. And he was the oldest of all the cousins, in his late thirties.

Just as my grandmother was running outside, something she never did, along with one of my mother's younger sisters, my grandfather pulled up.

My grandmother was visibly upset. I thought she was upset because my older cousin was fighting on younger me, but she was upset with me, her grandson, just because Buster Lee's eye was rolling around in the driveway. The passenger side of granddaddy's truck just missed the fake eye as he drove up.

My grandfather wasn't tripping...yet. He told us both to get inside. I didn't say anything. I just walked into the house feeling really bad after seeing his eye socket empty. My mother's sister didn't make it any better. She was cursing me out, too. Given that no one seemed interested at all in what actually happened, I started to feel stubborn.

Buster Lee immediately began to blame everything on me saying I initiated everything, even though I had a witness. Before this, I used to look up to him, but it hurt me so bad that he would lie on me like that when he should be setting an example. He had to know he was wrong.

With the way things were going, I decided I wouldn't even dignify anything with a response. I didn't care how scared of granddaddy I was supposed to be.

Hell, I was never scared of granddaddy anyway. When he asked me what happened, I said, "I ain't got nothing to say," and had the nerve to be aggravated when I said it.

He chimed, "Now wait a minute boy! Who you think you talking to?"

Still, I didn't respond and just stared at him intensely, dead in his eyes. I felt so proud that I refused to respond. I thought I was behaving honorably like my mother raised me to be. Besides, this shit was in my blood.

He started coming towards me and when I didn't budge, he attempted to hit me. I blocked his lick and the whole house got in an uproar claiming I raised my hand at Daddy. Well, I didn't mean to, and I can see how it appeared in retrospect, but they were wrong. Somebody I looked up to and respected, Buster Lee, had lied on me to protect his wrong. We were supposed to be family. This behavior was reserved for strangers.

My grandmother yelled out two words that would cut me for the rest of my life. "Get out!"

"Eric, you get out of here now!" she screamed, reiterating the same sentiments I heard when I left home in Dallas. "I don't care where you go, but you get out of here." I never ever heard my sweet lil' prissy grandmother raise her voice before.

Hurt, but proud, I didn't even get my belongings. I went outside and walked to the corner store to use the pay phone. That's where I met up with my homeboy who witnessed the whole thing. I told him what happened on the way to the pay phone. I had to call my mother and tell her what happened because I was sure they would have called her by now, giving her a reason to say "I told you so."

My mother listened to me until I was through and then said, "Do you know how to get to the bus station?"

I told her, "Yes ma'am." Note, now it is *yes ma'am* when responding to her. Somehow, I mustered up the proper amount of respect. There I was perturbed about treating family like strangers when in retrospect that was the way I had treated my mother. Life experiences have a way of doing that to you. Teaching you the same things that make you laugh can make you cry sometimes.

"Do you have your clothes?" mother said.

"No ma'am." Again, after being so cocky in the past, I found a sense of humbleness now.

"Go back and get yo' shit and nobody bet' not *say* nothing to you."

She didn't say "*do*" nothing to you, she went as far as to "say" nothing to you. Not that she could do anything way in Dallas, but that was just how we were. We believed everybody would do as *we* said. It was in our blood.

By the time I got back to the house, there they were and here they come. About ten of them were coming up the street with bats, sticks, purses, umbrellas and it wasn't even raining. Like I wasn't even kin to them. The head of the crew-slash-family were my cousins Barry Bee, Benny Gee, and Buster Lee; all three were brothers. They were coming down the street to jump on me. I couldn't believe it, but like I told you earlier I felt proud. I felt like I could whoop all them fools, so I boldly walked between all of them while they were talking shit, too. Straight down to my grandmother's house where I didn't even bother to go in to get my clothes. Instead, I sat across the street from my own grandmother's house on a curb.

They all came down the street and stood in the driveway across from me cacklin' about how I think I'm so bad and how I've been getting into fights since I got there.

"Ain't nobody gon' be scared of him," one of my aunts and female cousins had the gall to say.

I just sat there quietly, humbly, and proudly...and looked into each one of their eyes one by one.

They must've been scared. It's just lil' ole me...and all of them. Yet, nobody was jumping, which was fine by me. I would rather not fight with any of them, but right then and there, at that very moment, I think they would have gotten ten quick Mississippi Ass Whoopins'. All by me, one lil' Dallas ass whoppin' givin' mothaphucka.

The part that bothered me the most was my grandmother sitting in the window, just 'a watching. That was the loneliest part of the experience, but I also realized I had something they didn't have. I was the son of the Godfather's son...and they didn't do no talking. Unlike that side of the family who at times probably wasn't gon' bust a grape, my daddy's side of the family was gon' bust yo' ass and that too, was in my blood.

It all came down to mama, once again, saving the day. She didn't give a shit that they were her parents, sisters, nephews, nieces, and cousins. All she knew was she was **_my mama_** and I was her son. That meant us against the world, if need be. She didn't care how far apart we were...don't think about doing any harm to her son.

She went to a station in Dallas and paid for me a bus ticket. I used the money I already had to catch the bus to go to work and then catch the bus to the bus depot. Upon my arrival in Dallas, my mother was there waiting. I would always end up in a situation, but my mama was always there to bail me out. It's like no matter what I did or how far apart we were she always seemed to end up there...right there...every time.

CHAPTER 15

NOTHING LIKE THE BOND BETWEEN A MOTHER AND HER SON

My mother never did say those words *"I told you so."* It was still *"I love you son,"* so I really wasn't feeling her side of the family at all after that incident. I vowed never to go back to Mississippi again. I didn't care if I ever saw them again in life. Knowing my mother wouldn't approve of that, I never mentioned how I felt about them when we discussed everything in detail. She loved family, period! And especially hers. But that stubborn side of me came from my daddy's side.

Besides, she knew I was like that because she always called me ornery. I still didn't know what that meant exactly, but I had an idea.

When I got back home, I immediately enrolled in school. One problem though, it wasn't for me. It was for my mama because I was tired of disappointing her. I was gonna try to finish school and walk across that stage to get my diploma.

I also didn't want mama to look like a fool for coming to my rescue all the time. Our family already thought she answered my every beckon call...and in return I kept doing the same thing, fucking up.

Another reason I enrolled in school was because I didn't want to end up dead, like my daddy. I knew what was being said, "*She's ruining that boy. She's spoiling that boy. She's babying that boy. And none of that is going to help him be a man.*"

My mother's response to this talk was that she was a *single* parent and there was nothing like the bond between a mother and her son. Knowing she felt like that about me made me want to "big up"...a little, but no matter how hard I tried to walk the straight path, trouble always found me.

I wasn't at the school six weeks before the same ole niggas were hating on me again. They were from one of our cross-town rivalries. I starched their asses the two years I was at Westbury for a combined total of 438 rushing yards in three games, four touchdowns and 176 special teams' yards. Totaling out at 614 yards and four touchdowns.

I would be turning nineteen this year and was a year behind my class now. I was banking on the fact they probably had forgotten about me, but one of them remembered me from my old school. They weren't about to forget me with the couple of neighborhood tussles we'd been in. They didn't want to forget those either, so it was on.

This was the atmosphere I was becoming accustomed to since moving to Mississippi. I traded in my cleats for boxing gloves. They didn't know that Eric Payson was not known for running touchdowns anymore, but for kicking ass. However, just like me (and how I felt about the Raw Dawgs) they didn't give a shit. They stared, snarled, and one even had the nerve to say something.

"Say!" one of them bellowed out

I don't know who he talking to 'cause my name ain't say, I thought as I continued to eat my lunch. I had sense enough to know the mouthy one was just showing out. Plus, it wouldn't be smart to fight one of them because they all would jump in. But I'm Eric Payson, and like the rest of my family I can't stand the thought of somebody *thinking* I'm scared of them. Worse, I can't stand the thought of me feeling like it. Nevertheless, I continued eating.

"Say! Ain't you Eric Payson from Westbury?"

I looked up, well I didn't have to but I couldn't help it. I looked up slowly and over at him sitting about two cafeteria lunch tablets away. It's funny how amongst all that cafeteria chatter his was the only voice I heard.

I said, "You know who I am."

Every fork stopped going into mouths. Every milk stopped being drank. Everybody stopped talking. That's how quiet it got. All eyes were on me and this idiot who wanted to make me look like one.

"But do you know who I am?" he said.

"I don't recall asking you, so I don't give a shit who you are ."

Standing up, he replied, "I'm Percy Lee, nigga!" and started walking towards me.

I stood up and it seemed his whole football team got in between us. One said, *"Naw Percy, after school,"* and looked at me like we were friends or something. Then he said the same thing to me, "After school man. Is that cool?"

Oh how nice of you to ask, I thought. Since he did I answered, "Yeah, it's whatever."

I sat back down and continued eating. They went back to their side of the cafeteria high fivin' and laughing. Talking commenced amongst the rest of the noisy ass children in the cafeteria.

It wasn't a problem for me. I knew he would be getting his ass whopped. We even walked past each other a couple of times in the hallway on the way to classes, but this one time when I caught him by himself in the bathroom, oh yes! I couldn't help but confront him.

"Percy Lee, huh" You wanna get this over with right here?"

He was washing his hands with a smile on his face when he said, "Oh, you gon' steal off on me huh?"

"Naw, I don't get down like that. I'll whoop yo' ass fair and square."

"Yeah, and I'd rather whoop yo' ass in front of everybody," he said grabbing some paper towels to dry his hands, all while looking me dead in the eyes.

"No shit?"

"Noooo shit," he replied, as we got up on each other, nose to nose.

He dried his hands and we shook on it right there. I actually liked

Percy's style after that. He handled himself much like me. Grace under fire, cool under pressure. With only one more period to go before school was out everybody in class was asking, *"Eric you really gonna fight him?"* Like he was Mike Tyson or something. They didn't know that day I was gon' be Buster Douglas.

Come to find out, he was in a gang. My lil' sister who was now in the ninth grade had heard about it and came to my class to find out if it was true that I was gonna fight after school. I told her "naw" hoping she was just go on home after school, but out of fear she did not want to leave my side. She was gonna try to help me fight, I guess.

I told her "naw Bay-Bay we squashed it already."

She looked unsure as to whether or not I was telling the truth. When the bell rang, everybody was looking scared for me and wishing me well like this was gon' be their last time seeing me. I let their fear roll off like water to a duck.

Once I got outside my class, I saw that the school was emptying faster than a herd of cattle trying to get away from a rancher. All in a hurry to see me get my ass whooped.

We were to meet at the bridge. I could see the location of the bridge from where I was standing, but I couldn't see the bridge. It was that packed, on both sides of the street. One of my childhood friends whose house I used to stay over during my little league years just happened to attend the same school. He caught up with me on my way to the bridge to try to warn me that they were all going to jump on me.

"It is not going to be one on one Eric," he told me with the same fear that the kids in my last period class had.

I was grateful for the information, but it was too late. I had already made a pact to fight him. Wasn't no turning back now. My little league potna begged me not to go with tears in his eyes. I appreciated the sentiments, but what I needed right now was somebody to pump me up not this bitch ass shit.

I took off my Westbury letterman jacket and told him to hang on to it and proceeded to walk to the bridge by myself. A few latecomers were following close behind, but half the school was already waiting with their popcorn. I approached the bridge and the street parted like the Red Sea. I felt like a gladiator fighting for my life and prepared to die for it.

As the street cleared, Percy Lee stood front and center with his arms opened as if to give me a hug, smiling with confidence. I took my shirt off and he took off his. Without as much as a word exchanged we engaged! I immediately caught him with my signature three piece. BING! BING! BING!, one – two - three crisp Hiram Clarke jabs to the face and one to the ribs that knocked him off balance. He then did the unthinkable. He rushed me like a mad bull with his head down. I was unable to move out of his way, but there's no wrestling in fighting, he knew this.

While he was about to ram me, I was thinking *now this nigga is scared, I'm gon' whoop him after three punches,* and he never was able to take a swing yet.

His homeboys must've thought I was gon' whoop him too because they did just like my lil' homie suggested...stomped the shit out of me. I balled up in a knot, but kept an eye out to see who actually was kicking me, and it was all of them.

The part that killed me was that my lil' sister went with her instincts and decided to come back up to the school. Unfortunately stumbling upon her big brother getting "smashed on" in the middle of a four-way intersection. She didn't come unprepared. She had a piece of closet pole with her and didn't hesitate to start swingin' that som' bitch either. One of the niggas picked my lil' sister up and the next thing I knew she was doing a helicopter spin through the air onto some sticker bushes.

Aw hell naw!! I found some way to get up from the bottom of that pile. Got up and came out swinging like a mad man.

Next thing I heard was...**pow!-pow!**

Two shots rang out and everybody running every which a way. My only concern was my lil' sister at that point.

Then there wasn't anyone left but me and my lil' sister standing in the middle of the street. It was quiet as that lunchroom earlier that day. Then I felt a warm feeling running down my midsection. I looked down and saw blood. I had been shot in the stomach just above my belt buckle. I sat on the curb not wanting my lil' sister to panic.

I calmly said, "Bay- Bay. You got to go call an ambulance, alright. I will be alright."

She took a glance at the blood and immediately ran off.

All I kept saying was, "I'm gon' get'em, I'm gon' get'em." Like I was sure my daddy felt. It never crossed my mind about dying, but I didn't want to look directly at my wounds though. I didn't want to know how bad it was.

Suddenly, a vehicle was coming down the street. As it got near me, it began to slow down. I immediately became suspect when the car got right up on me and came to a complete stop.

It was a black Lincoln Continental weighed down in the back with limousine tint on it. When the window rolled down half way, it was Percy Lee. I braced myself because I knew he was getting ready to finish me off. My whole life passed in front of me. All the mistakes I made. All the situations I made myself vulnerable to. All the adversities I subjected my family to. Now this! My mother would have to find me either out of breath on this curb...or dead in the street. Not exactly how I planned it. In fact, I would end up just like my daddy.

Then, I heard his voice and could not believe what I was hearing. His mystical voice was comforting in the midst of this turmoil.

"Say man, I didn't mean for it to go down like that. We shook on it and my word is my bond. This here is the punk ass nigga that shot you?"

The window rolled down some more and I recognized that it was one of his younger homies trying to make rank with that dumb ass cowboy move.

"Yeah man," I answered faintly.

"Eric, you can shoot this ho yo' self or we will take care of this nigga. That's on erry' thang big homie," Percy Lee said.

Hearing that, I really liked the cat for real then. "Big homie" meant they now respected me. Percy Lee reminded me a lot of myself. Only difference was he had a full scholarship waiting for him so he had no reason to be caught up in this foolishness.

"Naw I'm straight, but when I get well... we gon' have to finish this."

He said, "No doubt big homie. No doubt."

The sirens rang out in the distance. Opening the car door, he pointed to his leg and said, "Fine but if it makes you feel any better, when I get well too. This fool ass nigga accidentally shot me too. We're on our way to the hospital. You wanna ride?"

I quickly declined, sounded too much like right. Fearing already I would end up like my daddy by the time I was twenty-three. They weren't going to end up driving me around until I bled to death and drop me off on my mama's porch. The ambulance and local authorities pulled up along with my uncle, sister, and Ms. Belinda. Another ambulance had taken my mother to the hospital already.

When my sister told my mother what happened to us, my mother passed out. My sister called an ambulance for my mother and when one arrived she told them about me, so they dispatched another. That's what took them so long. Once I heard about mama that was all I was concerned about, my mother. Until I started to feel sleepy and weak.

I woke up in the recovery room after emergency surgery to remove a bullet lodged in my right kidney. All I wanted to know was if my mother was okay. When I was stable enough to get the news, the doctor told me that my mother had a mild stroke that may have done some damage to her kidneys and heart. She would have to stay in the hospital for some tests and rest.

In return, I was home in a couple of days. I prayed and prayed and prayed for her health. Confused as to how and why I would and could get shot in my kidneys, and it be okay. Yet my mother not be shot in hers and both be damaged.

I was mad with God, and when I would visit my mother in the hospital all she was concerned with, was me. She wanted to know was I doing okay, healing up properly and how soon could she get home to take care of me.

"Why Lord? Why would you do this to my mama?" I whispered one evening when I thought mama was sleep.

She immediately corrected me and told me, "Baby please don't question God. He has a master plan and he is never wrong."

She encouraged me to read my Bible more, saying "You're 'bout to enter into adulthood now and become a young man in the world. I may not always be here, so you should know the Word for yourself, baby."

I placed my head on her belly and just cried. I asked the Lord if he could just let my mama be alright and told him I would do right. I prayed every day and night. Even went to church for a couple of Sundays with my grandmother.

Finally my mama was released from the hospital to come home. Though initially they thought she might need to be put on dialysis, she was okay and couldn't have been more grateful.

By this time, I was too far behind to stay in school, but for the remainder of the time in school those cats loved me because they couldn't believe I didn't tell the authorities anything. Yeah, I guess I was like my daddy and never told who shot me either. All I wanted to do was get them back, but I promised God I would do right. And that was on my mama, so they got a pass from me... and my mama. In return because of that, I guess I got one from them. Gives a whole new meaning to do unto others as you would have them do unto you, don't it?

...But how about Eric Jerome Payson just not doing nothing unto anybody for a while? Could he manage that one first?

CHAPTER 16

MARK MY WORDS

I tried to find a job with no luck, so once again I was hanging out a lot at Nikki's. Eventually, I ended up taking a test for the Army and passed with flying colors. I wanted to learn how to fly helicopters, but needed college hours to do so. As a result my M.O.S. ended up being a dental hygienist. It was either that or M.P. (military police). I chose dental hygienist because I could leave for basic training right away in May. It was already January and MP didn't have a class again until October.

Excited about my new moves, I began making plans with Nikki. She was ready to leave home too. I didn't tell my family until about two weeks before I was to leave.

Me and mama already were butting heads again. She was real irritated that I hadn't gone back to school...yet, so I gave in and told her my plans. It was time for me to go and I was ready to leave.

This time I wasn't coming back. Unfortunately before I left, my mother got a call in the middle of the morning, as did my grandmother at 4 a.m. That never was good. Being all the men seemed to not come in until the wee hours of the morning for long as I could remember. A call like that could only mean one thing. My grandfather had been murdered, he was shot point-blank range three times in the back of his head.

"The Black Godfather is Gone" is what the front page of a local black newspaper read. Someone had gotten that close to him, which he normally didn't allow. The only clue the police had was that it was probably someone he knew and trusted to allow them that close to him.

My grandmother was terribly distraught because like every other situation nobody knew anything...anytime...every time.

That was the lifestyle my grandfather chose to live...and the one my lil' Christian grandmother chose to deny, obviously. It had come full circle— charge it to the game, they would come to say.

My grandfather's funeral was an immaculate event with heads of state in the pews, the mayor, city councilmen, entertainers local and abroad to charity event organizers, and non-profit organization heads to little league referees, and boys club kids. I never ever saw white people up close like that unless it was at a hospital or jail. I mean these were some big wigs. Of course, all of the gamblers and hustlers came out...all the way from Cali and Vegas.

The funny thing was no one in the streets ever knew my grandfather was married. My mother said my grandmother found out my grandfather had another woman that they knew in the streets. Her name was Nona. She was just his ho to me. Finding out about her made me not feel so bad that he was dead. He hurt my grandmother. Even still, I wasn't able to separate the pride I had being his grandson.

My grandmother ended up going to court behind a lot of his properties. The club where he was shot at. The restaurant he just opened. And my grandfather's pride and joy, the car lot. Nona was trying to contest everything like she was really his wife.

Do you know my grandmother signed everything over to the courts, except her house that they lived in and her one Cadillac Seville, saying she didn't want any parts of anything that had something to do with Nona? Even another big house that my grandfather purchased for him and Nona, and a brand new Candy Apple Red Cadillac he recently purchased that the killers who shot him drove into the bayou. He also recently had won a brand new Corvette off a Super Bowl pot, an event he also attended with

Nona.

My grandmother didn't care. Her lil' modest house with all of that fancy funeral home furniture was all she was concerned with. She never wanted a big house, though she could've had one. She was very conservative in contrast to my grandfather who was a flashy som' bitch.

At the funeral was the first time my grandmother saw me preoccupied with a female. Nikki was by my side the whole time. She and I were planning a life together, so it was time they all got used to her. My grandmother, though cordial to Nikki, did not approve at all.

Before I left she asked me, "Is that the lil' girl you plan on marrying."

I said, "Yes mama." I called her mama too.

Though she much was shorter than me, she lifted my chin up to look me in the eyes. Whenever I was around her, I felt nine years old all over again and had a tendency to look towards the ground.

"That lil' girl is trouble boy."

I was afraid to respond, but I said, "You don't know that."

"Mark my words, ya' hear." Grandma stared at my pitiful looking self and then hugged me and added, "Good God Almighty, love ya' to death boy!"

When it came to me and my brother, she always ended things like that. She kissed me on my mouth with her little perched lips and smiled with that big "gate mouf" smile just like mine.

All I could think was *damn! That look just like my smile.* I was proud of that blood I had in me, but didn't like to go around them because I didn't feel like I was living up to it. All of that was about to change.

My grandmother, however, never knew how much that statement would effect me. Neither would I. But then again, it being my grandmother, maybe she did.

CHAPTER 17

DON'T LET THE JOKE BE ON YOU

Every time I saw Nikki, my grandmother's words would enter my head. How could she be so sure about someone she never met. I blew it off as another family member being narrow minded 'cause she had a daughter already, talked back to adults, smoked weed and cigarettes, and didn't finish high school. Seemed like the perfect match to me. That's why I chose to marry her, we both were degenerates.

However, I wanted to establish myself a bit more before we got married, so the wedding would have to wait until after basic training. That was at least sixteen weeks away.

Before I left I had a few difficulties. First mama got very upset because she didn't find out I was leaving until the last minute. She got even more upset knowing that Nikki knew all along. Even worse, Nikki decided to tell her we were getting married. Let me repeat, Nikki decided to. Mind you, they were not close at all. She didn't ask, nor tell, me she was going to do so.

Adamant, my mother thought this was some fatal attempt by a lil' wicked, evil, and fast-ass hussy to throw it up in her face that she had her son...or would have him soon. *I think not.* Hell, we "*were*" getting married, so it could've been, maybe, just maybe that Nikki was excited.

NOPE!

She knew how my mother would react, which is why I didn't want to tell her yet. I knew she would object. Not only that – I told Nikki not to say anything to anyone, so I was suspect as well. I was upset that she hurt my mother.

My mother begged me not to marry her, so I told her I wouldn't and I meant that. I called it off with Nikki and then she begged me not to call it off. I wasn't sure anymore so I played it by ear. Sometimes to shut up Nikki, I would say *"yea, we are still going to get married, but don't mention it to nooo-body."*

One weekend, when I was supposed to come home after about ten weeks into basic training and after ten weeks of saying we are getting married and then reneging, Nikki went ahead and made plans without informing me. She must've gotten tired of the back-and-forth and became suspect about it, so this time she had everything set up to tie the knot. I came home on a pass. I didn't have to travel far because I was stationed at Ft. Bliss in El Paso, Texas, a few hours in flight time to Dallas.

Being the sucker I was for Nikki, we ended up getting married anyway. One thing didn't happen though. I didn't tell my grandmother. She wasn't at the lil' makeshift wedding at a friend of my mother's house. She probably wouldn't have attended anyway. I'm telling you, we are ornery like that on that side.

As if things could get worse, before the honeymoon got started good, Nikki got pregnant. I was excited about having a lil' boy. Before the child was born, I was planning on having a son. I mean, I was singing to her belly and the baby, buying Oshkosh and bringing home shit for the baby every single weekend. I even bought a big wheel and a red tricycle. I actually was happy and proud of the progress I was making towards becoming a man. At this point, my mother and Nikki were getting along fairly well and I finally got around to telling my grandmother about the marriage and the baby on the way.

My defining moment came when she was about to have the baby. I caught a flight and made it home just in time. I was surprised to see everybody there, my family and hers. Never in my wildest dreams did I imagine companionship could be this bliss between two. That day, I found out having a baby together really cements the bond between a couple.

That was until that baby's head poked out and it was a baby girl, and it was the splitting image of Kiki, Nikki's first born for that old ass nigga she claimed not to know where he was at.

But oh, she knew alright. She knew where he was every night while I was in basic training at Bivwack, as in the military. Preparing to risk my life to build one for her like my mother begged me not to. Like my grandmother warned me about. Like my gut left me suspicious about the whole time I knew her black ass. My whole world sank at the thought that the baby might not be mine. That alone, I could have lived with, but why did it have to be him again?

After requesting a blood test, the baby ended up not being mine at all. It was for that other old ass nigga Nikki admitted.

My mind was in overdrive! I was livid about the baby. How could this have happened? I mean, I put my faith, my love, and my loyalty into Nikki. She didn't have to do this. Not this. I could've dealt with the fooling around, but not getting pregnant with another man's baby while I'm pledging my love to you. My grandmother told me so. She told me that lil' girl was too fast for me. I even left home for her and joined the military to help support her and Kikki.

Not only did my mother tell me about Nikki, but the one person I would hate to face at a time like this...with something as devastating as this. I wouldn't want to be the one to disclose this info because I'd have to look her in the face and tell the truth, and admit that I was wrong and she was right.

Attempting to distance myself from Nikki by annulling our marriage, gave me some solace. I thought my mother would be more upset than anyone, but she had a soft spot for females like Nikki for some reason. I assumed it was because they reminded her of herself in some ways or simply she could relate to the situation. She took to Nikki, consoled her, molded her, and walked with her through this...never letting go of her hand.

My sister on the other hand was gonna make sure I never forgot what that "bitch," as she would refer to her so eloquently, did to me.

Or forget what a "bitch" like her looked like. I couldn't understand. I was supposed to think all bitches looked like Nikki or Nikki looked like all bitches...nevertheless I didn't need any reminders. I was never going to forget how someone betrayed my love like that. It seemed to be my life's story. Somebody trading my love in for another man.

It started with my mama, then Ms. Belinda, and now Nikki. Nikki desperately wanted to salvage our relationship, but I wasn't willing. I had one thing on my mind, seeing my grandmother and being honest about things to her for a change– and not her being honest with me. I wanted to initiate it, and not have her lift my chin up like I was a kid and look the truth up out me...or speak it into me.

Before I could do any of that though, I had to deal with the trouble my mindset got me in.

I began to get very belligerent apparently. Disobedient to authority and downright rebellious. I would get into so much trouble until they eventually discharged me from the Army. Even Uncle Sam didn't want to have anything to do with my ass.

During my time in the military, I never did muster up the courage it took to look my grandmother in the face after Nikki and I divorced. It had been a year since I last saw her.

My attitude really became shitty. I guess all that honorable talk about integrity was out the window and it showed in my behavior.

I was fighting all the time now, late to every roll call. Forgery and fraud followed suit. Being docked of my whole paycheck, not to mention the numerous AWOLs. I violated so much I was confined to the base for one year after I violated that agreement by going AWOL again. I was put on what you call police detail. Normally, this meant just staying late, clearing and policing the area, but for me, Eric Jerome Payson, it meant painting every dental clinic on the base before I would be court marshaled or discharged. Nine dental clinics needed to be painted inside and out before my three months were to expire. Not a major problem...but I wasn't a painter or carpenter. I took it to mean they didn't care how those clinics were painted.

I began my detail in clinic number one. I took that roller, dipped it in that paint and did just that. I began rolling that bad boy...all up and down that wall...ever which-a-way. Not the proper way, I'm assuming by the way the military police were looking and laughing at me every evening, on the cool, when they came by to check on me to make sure I was at my specified post at my specified time. 1800 hours (6:00 p.m.) every afternoon, I was to report without fail. I worked in the dental clinic from 8 a.m. to 5 p.m., got one hour to go to chow and be at my post by 6 p.m. 'til 10 p.m. with paintbrush in hand...stroking.

So the proper way was to roll the brush straight up and down evenly as one of the MPs attempted to instruct me, for my benefit. Little did he know, or come to find out, I took pride in my fucking up those military walls. I acted as though I had no idea I was doing anything wrong. Stroking that brush in a "Z" formation like I was Zorro. Then up and down and back to a 45-degree angle. I even painted in a couple of circle formations.

Those MPs looked at me work like they saw a ghost. Undoubtedly, they went back and told my first sergeant about my handy work and he obviously wasn't pleased. Problem was, no one ever told me he wasn't. Nooooooooo! They allowed me to spend time painting every dental clinic for sixty-five days, inside and out, with that Barnum and Bailey Circus painting routine I had the nerve to put on.

Everyone, I'm talking about everyone checkin' on me everyday! When I thought I was done... when there were only fifteen days left for them to make a determination on my future. And fifteen days until I thought I was going back into the free world, my friends and maybe my girl, they hit me with it. They called me up to that office and knocked all the wind out of me.

"Private Eric Jerome Payson, you are still here but confined to the barracks C143-86 for the remainder of your tour of duty or until your assignment has been completed!"

I replied, "But I did, I painted all those dental clinics."

My Sergeant Major looked like he was doing everything he could to hold his composure.

"That you did. That you did. Only this time, you will paint them all right. At ease private." He dismissed me.

"Sir. Yes sir."

A familiar voice came to my thoughts. *Remember Eric. You can always tell jokes...but it ain't good to be the butt end of 'em.* That was something I seemed to be good at...becoming the butt end of my own jokes.

CHAPTER 18

TIME TO FACE THE MUSIC

Got damn! My grandmother always used to stay, *"Eric, it's okay to joke...but make sure the joke ain't on you."*

Shame, confused and angry, I somehow thought it would take me 65 days to paint 9 dental clinics. Wrong! That was without any effort or paying attention to detail, but it would take twice as long to do it right.

Actually, I learned something in this. It doesn't take as long to do things *right the first time*. It takes longer when you fuck up and have to go back and redo what you've already done. Another thing grandmother used to always say. I knew then that I would have to face my grandmother, but it hurt to even think about looking into her eyes. There was no way around it. It was time to face the music.

Man, I didn't give a damn. I was so relieved to leave that damn military base it wasn't funny. I didn't care about all that being all you could be or none of that. I just wanted out.

I planned on isolating myself and becoming reclusive to the point that for a while I didn't tell anyone I was even kicked out the Army. Embarrassed mostly, I guess.

I was twenty years old and all I had to show for it was nothing. At every corner, I ruined a good thing – almost deliberately. I knew it was me, but I was in denial. 'Cause I sure was behaving like it was the world's fault.

My mother and Nikki, on the other hand, formed a perfect mother-daughter relationship. After two years, they were getting along and the baby still came around all the time. I never understood their relationship, but my mama was confronting me all the time attempting to get me to understanding females, especially Nikki, and situations like this. I was not trying to hear that female bullshit. How about I get y'all to understanding men and the way we process y'all's bullshit? Kerry express this a little further or omit it. Yeah, if I was one or could become one. But I am still full of shit...bullshit at that. You are what you eat huh?(shuddup!)

Once again, I couldn't find a job and the dishonorable discharge on my record was not helping me any. When I did get work I ended up getting arrested for unlawfully carrying a weapon on the premises, which was a lesser charge from what it could have been. They gave me two years probation thinking I would learn my lesson. Only for me to leave the gun in my car at work and take it inside the club and get busted with it again.

Violating my probation, how dumb was that? Dumb enough to land the rest of the two years in jail.

Could've been worse, but as my grandmother would say, *"Eric, you always had angels watching over you boy. You been a blessed child all yo' life."* Yet and still, I begged to differ. If that was what being blessed was about, count me out grandmother. She was right though, and that was one of the reasons I never called her whenever I was in trouble. I was ashamed. Ashamed to be her grandson...and not being a man...because I felt my actions brought shame to her.

Me and my mother weren't communicating as much. Half of the time she never knew what city I was getting in trouble with the law in. Another indication that I was doing something I had no business was I stayed away from family when I was like that. What was I running from?

Mama came to see me every other weekend and kept a letter

or two in the mail from everybody. I knew I should've been more grateful. I should've said thank you for being there and keeping me company in jail the whole time. They kept money on my books. I never wanted for nothin'. What did I do to show my thanks? Get out and go right back to jail. Three months out and I get into a fight with none other than Nikki.

I had nowhere to go when I got out of jail, so Nikki and I hooked back up. Of course, without the blessings of mama. She was totally against it...I mean livid and opposed to it. Even though she and Nikki had formed a bond, she did not think it was wise for us to get back together.

Nikki wanted to show me that she could be faithful and how much she loved me, but every time I looked at that lil' baby girl I would despise her very existence. I couldn't take the relationship seriously.

Still being a coward, I never told my grandmother ever. I didn't want to face her so I stayed away from my grandmother, even after I heard she was ill. Mama was so upset with me and Nikki that she stopped associating with Nikki. She thought I wasn't ready for a relationship, saying, "You are too volatile and possibly institutionalized."

"*Institutionalized!*" What was she talking about? I had only been to jail three times, and two times was in the last three months. I was only there two years.

CHAPTER 19

I'M GON' LEARN

It didn't take long before Nikki and I were at each other's throats again. I wasn't in love anymore and she was more possessive than ever. Not only that, she was big as a house. So I wasn't attracted to her at all. I just needed somewhere to lay my head down when I got home from prison. I only stayed as long as I did just to spite mama and to possibly prove she wasn't right about me. It seemed as though she always was right.

During my stay with Nikki, I became somewhat violent and very physically abusive towards her. There was something about Nikki though. She seemed to get excited at the thought of the after thought each time we fought. Her eyes would light up, boy would they light up!

Her pupils would begin to dilate and I could see the blood rushing through her veins. It seemed like her pressure would rise. Initially, it was a turn on, but eventually it became disgusting...once I realized why we were fighting. Always over nothing. She just wanted to get a rise out of me, and I do mean that in more ways than one. At any rate, for me, that got old fast.

Once I realized what she was doing, that made things worse for us both. Her because she would tolerate anything as long as I got on top of her afterwards. Worse for me because I didn't want to be there anyway.

'Til one day, we were driving down the road and the anger began to form. Rage was mounting, suddenly an adrenalin rush came up out of the blue. It was like the devil recorded and kept pressing rewind in my head of the catastrophes of my past with Nikki. I imagined all the time I spent desiring her, chasing her, helping her and wanting to love her and I began to look back on where I went wrong. What was wrong with my life? Why did I feel so trapped? And it all came to me.

> You spited your mother and grandmother for this bitch. Trying to prove them wrong just cause yo' dumb selfish ass wasn't right. At every corner, you spited, disobeyed and ignored their cries. You had a fresh start going into the military, going for her when you wouldn't have gone for yourself. But that didn't pan out, the marriage , the baby, nor the military, so you traded all three for prison. Why? Because you didn't do it for you...any of it! You did it for her...all of it!. And what did she do to show her appreciation? She had a mothaphuckin' baby for another nigga , again while she was planning to marry and claiming to LOVE YOU!!!.

And that is when it happened. Out of nowhere, filled with power surge and rage...**SLLAAPP!!** across her face without any warning. I mean, a gigantic, backhanded SLAP smack dab in the middle of her face!

We had been merely driving quietly because I hated to talk to her since it always felt like she was bothering me, so I admit the rage was rather sudden.

Simultaneously while smacking her in the face, I blurted out, "Bitch, you ruined my life!"

Caught completely off guard, she let out a frantic yell and her facial expression quickly went from happy-go-lucky to shock and disbelief. I pulled my arm back with a closed fist. This time, I was going to punch her in the face, but a "whoop-whoop" sound followed by flicker of lights appeared in my rear view mirrors. Red, white and blue in succession blinded me as I caught my snap.

Nikki was crying profusely by then. I was sure she was confused, but then so was I.

I was confused too as to where, why and what made me just unleash that fury on her like that. Tell you what though, I was gonna have plenty of time to think about it with that red, white and blue flickering in my rearview. It was the police.

Thinking about not stopping at all for a minute, I pleaded with Nikki to stop crying. "Baby please, you got to get yourself together. Come on Nikki. Don't send me back to jail baby, I'm sorry."

I could tell she was so hurt, embarrassed and confused. She just kept saying, "I never meant to hurt you, I love you. I love you Eric."

By then, the officer was on his intercom. "Pull the vehicle over now!"

I pleaded with her. "C'mon baby. I'm gon' get some help. I'm losing it and I ain't got nothing."

She was still crying and couldn't seem to pull herself together. The idea of going back to jail was paralyzing me at that point. I mean I really was not thinking too rational, but my grandmother and mother's face seemed to show up out of nowhere. Their voices told me the right thing to do was to pull over Eric and face the music.

"*You been running too long. Time to take responsibility for your actions Eric,*" were their exact mystical sentiments. They weren't fussing, just calmly reminding me. It felt like angels were wrapping their arms around me.

A calm came over me and I pulled the car over. There were two officers that came up on both sides of the vehicle with flashlights.

"Sir, step out of the vehicle."

"For what officer?" I was a little nervous, so I took my time unhooking my seatbelt and preparing to exit the car.

"I saw you striking the young lady on the passenger side." The officer on my side motioned with his hand for me to step out of the car.

Still crying uncontrollably, Nikki blurted out, "He wasn't striking me. It was a spider in my hair and he was striking at the spider." I looked over at her like I couldn't believe what I was hearing.

The officer insisted, "Ma'am, you don't have to lie. I know what I saw."

Suddenly, her crying ceased completely. Obviously irritated at the fact he was gon' tell her what happened when she said it didn't. That was enough to piss her off and halt her crying. "How you gon' tell me what it was, when I'm telling you he didn't hit me?" she screamed with conviction.

Meanwhile, I was getting ready to get out of the car for the officers, but Nikki said, "Don't get out Eric. If he ain't under arrest he ain't got to get out."

It was quiet as a church mouse on that busy street with oncoming traffic, wind, and 18-wheelers. I couldn't hear any of that at that moment. I was listening to see who was right. 'Cause I desperately needed Nikki to be right in this case.

The officers looked at each other and the one at my door side implied sarcastically, " Did you get the spider?"

Taking a deep breath, I watched him focus on the lie about to come out of my mouth.

"Yes sir...I believe so. We are headed to a nearby car wash now to vacuum the car out."

"Get the fuck out of here, boy!" he replied, obviously pissed because he knew the truth but couldn't do anything about it without Nikki's consent.

He didn't have to tell me twice. I drove off into the night, quietly, not saying a word. I felt awfully guilty and confused, so I waited for her to go to sleep that night and then quietly collected my belongings and left without saying a word. Same thing make you laugh, make you cry...up in hur, up in hur...still.

"I'm' gon' learn. I'm gon' learn."

CHAPTER 20

YOU GON' KILL YO MAMA

As you can see, I love to get in trouble I can't get out of and still ain't taking responsibility. Still blaming or looking for someone to blame for my fuck ups.

I wasn't gon' stay around there and wake up to a gang of police like Bryan Terry did in Kerry E. Wagner's first National Best Seller "*She Did That. (shuddup!)*" Un huh! I was gon' learn my lesson. At least I hoped.

Nikki frantically paged me all morning. I didn't return her pages, merely trying to avoid her to keep from causing any more complications. Plus, I didn't want to hear all of that crying and shit. It was what was best, I thought, because I didn't trust myself around her. But my pager was blowing up!

Just my luck later that day after not answering her calls all day, I started receiving pages from my sister also. I finally got the nerve to answer and got the surprise of my life.

My mother, after finding out about the altercation, had a stroke and was rushed to the hospital. She was in the critical care unit and my entire family was there, apparently.

I didn't know what to do. I thought my mother would die so I couldn't bring myself to see her like that. Not only that, it was "because of me" my sister and aunt would say.

"Eric you killing mama with yo' bullshit!" my sister said when I finally answered her page. And it kept playing over and over in my head until it was suffocating.

I kept imagining her at the hospital with tubes running in and out of her. I couldn't do it.

Two months!...Two months, my mother was in that hospital and three of those weeks in intensive care and not once did I go up there to see her. My family was furious with me and my selfishness because my mother was known to have done anything for me. She ended up losing her kidneys as a result of the stroke and me and my run ins with the police.

Even though this time I wasn't arrested, it was the thought of the incident that was too much for mama to bear. The older she got, the less able her feeble body was able to handle me and my foolishness.

What did she do until her body was too weak and tired to withstand the angst? Night after night, she prayed and prayed... waited and waited...to either see me or hear from me...and where was I? Nowhere to be found, but mama would do just as my daddy's mama would do. That apple ain't fall too far from the tree on this one.

My mother dreaded getting that fatal call in the middle of the night that her one and only son was dead. Killed in the street in the wee hours of the night.

I didn't mean to be selfish. I was just afraid, ashamed and consumed with guilt. I didn't go see my mother until she was released and being nursed at my aunt's house.

I was the last one to arrive, as usual. High and drunk from my pity party with myself. I just knew everybody was gonna be bitching at me. I stood at the door and took one last swig of Old English.

When the door opened, my sister took the bottle from me, gave me a sisterly hug and said, "C'mon in here and see yo' mama Eric."

I walked in tentatively, pacing and still afraid, ashamed as I went. My sister took her hand and put it in the small of my back, nudging and urging me forward. I left my shades on, which we weren't allowed to do in the house. I didn't want to make eye contact with anyone.

Finally, as I turned the corner and the living room parts like the red sea with all eyes on me, I saw mama. I didn't even recognize her until she said, "There go my baby!"

Her face was swollen, three times the usual size. Hair was all over her face. She almost looked like an ape. Her lips were pink and red and her skin was dark. I cried like a baby as she reached out for me to come to her from her seat. I couldn't believe that was my mama. I was crying because I was shame to not have seen her while she was sick. And I was shame because I was scared of how she looked.

She hugged me and said, "I'm alright baby, mama alright."

I couldn't control it after that. My crying was uncontrollable. The fact that here she was the one who had been suffering. The one that was sick. The one that was on her deathbed just days ago. Yet, she still was worrying, concerned and consoling me. Still consoling me... Still consoling me.

CHAPTER 21

GET YO SHIT TOGETHER ERIC

I wondered why nobody bothered me about not going to see mama when she was sick. My family was notorious about getting in someone's ass. But it was my mother who forbade it before I got there. Well, she forbade it in front of her, but not while she wasn't around because my sister and auntie couldn't wait for mama not to be around. They lit into my ass. I could'a swore I wasn't family. I was every kind of selfish mothaphucka in the book. Typically, I wouldn't even swear with the women in my family, but this time I did.

Even after that visit, I still wasn't coming around helping out enough or at all. I didn't like seeing her like that. Her spirit was well. She had good energy or appeared to be in good spirits. But no!

"She is putting up a good front for you, Eric. So you can be comfortable and won't be afraid to come see her. You are all she talks about. You are the one she wants to come visit and help her. She needs you," my sister scolded me.

Well, that only made me feel worse. Telling me that didn't help at all. I got in the girl's car I was driving to get over there that night. 'Cause I still didn't have shit. I didn't even have my own car, which was another reason I felt like shit around there. Everybody else was being responsible, had a job, if not a good one, or a career.

What did I have? A lil' ole temp job ever now and then with no benefits paying only about fifty dollars a day. After I ate and rode the bus or put gas in whatever girl I was seeing at the time's gas tank I was broke again by the next time I got up to go to work. Not the manliest thing to me.

Eventually, my mother was the one to break down her situation. After three years of dialysis treatments, she finally caught up with me and explained everything. She knew I loved her, with everything in me. I was raised like that, and not only that, it was in my genes. She basically revealed to me all my thoughts through this conversation. She knew it was shame, guilt and irresponsibility that made me weary of seeing her when she was at her most vulnerable state.

I began to cry again, uncontrollably. She attempted to console me as usual, but I hated feeling like that. I hated crying when I was supposed to be so hard. Crying made me sink more into my guilt and pity.

I immediately did as I usually did. Jumped into whatever girl's car I was seeing at the time and burnt the fuck off, fish tailing all the way up the road. I planned on staying away from everybody.

It was no use. I wasn't gon' amount to nothing, so I wasn't gon' feel like nothing, it felt suicidal. Especially when my mother needed me most. At least, she had the rest of my family. She would be okay.

I planned not to even go to the funeral, if she died. Not that I didn't want to, but if I couldn't stand seeing her sick and suffering, I knew I couldn't have dealt with seeing her in a casket. Oh no! And I still hadn't conquered that fear completely yet. Remember, I had been tortured by dead people and caskets since my days as a little boy back at my grandmother's house – who I had not seen and had not planned on seeing until I got my shit together. I was in no hurry to see her either.

I was half grown, but her and all that fancy ass funeral home furniture still didn't sit well with me. I didn't even know how she was doing, but her I didn't worry about. No matter how old she was getting that was somebody I knew wasn't gon' ever die. She was that strong and invincible as far as I was concerned.

But that got me to thinking. What if my grandmother found out, which I knew she had? She was God, or at least knew Him or Her personally. She knew everything, and I do mean everything without anybody telling her...but God. That one thought at that time was enough to get my brain churning. It always crossed my mind. What my grandmother would say to me or what that look in her eyes while lifting my chin up to look her in hers would do to me, whenever she and I finally had to face off? I had been avoiding that, and her, for years but even I began to realize something. *You can run, but you can't hide, Eric Payson.*

I also realized that like my daddy, constantly causing worry, concern and eventually grief to his mama and grandmother I was doing the same thing, possibly. I was killing my mama with misery and grief over my unstableness, irresponsibility, and carelessness. It was that moment I decided I had to get it right. And, just maybe, I could save my mother's life and mine too in the process.

She was becoming very ill. Tired of going to dialysis places and being unable to do things for herself. No traveling or enjoying life no more...just "getting busy dying" because she was unable to live.

Redemption came to mind. Maybe I could redeem myself as a son. Then that would redeem me as a grandson. Then that would redeem me as a man and that would redeem me as a person. I had heard of killing two birds with one stone. But had anyone ever killed four? This would be my new goal. My grandmother probably would forgive me for having the courage and resiliency to take that negative and turn it into a positive as she always preached about.

I put my plan together for my future. First thing I'm gon' do is get a real job. I mean really look. Like get up every morning at 6 a.m. and be the first one on the bus out looking. I'm gon' get serious about life and the people I cherish the most. Have me a plan and a strategy, set out to execute and not give up until I succeed.

I'm gon' be somebody. More than that, I'm gon' be a son and grandson. I'm gon be what I was put here to be, and mama and grandma...they are gon' see...they gon' live to see it and be proud of it if I have anything to do with it.

CHAPTER 22

GOD HAS THE FINAL WORD

I was still alienating everyone because I just didn't feel good about myself...yet Feeling very inadequate considering everything that was going on, ya' know? But a stroke of good luck during some bad luck would come my way unfortunately. Or is that fortunately?

Unfortunately or fortunately, I ended up getting a job. Yeah, I was riding with a girlfriend of mine, well one of 'em, in her brand new Ford Escort. She was giving me a ride to the other side of town. I wanted to use her car, again, but her mother had just helped her get a new vehicle with insurance and everything so she wasn't about to let me start putting miles on this one like I had done the last one she let me drive everyday and tear up.

Besides I wasn't going to look for no job. It was the weekend and I was going to my potna's house to play some dominoes. Not to smoke or drank, well not so much of that at least. I was trying to cut back on my bad habits. Though I wasn't going to see my mother still because I was shame, I was calling and communicating more.

Not only was it lifting her spirits up, it was lifting mine as well.

Man, I couldn't believe how upbeat she would be after those long three and four hour dialysis sessions. She would often tell me how she would cramp up, sometimes faint or just be plain exhausted after those sessions. Not to mention, she could be hell on wheels, giving those nurses hell. Not about herself but the other patients. Be it from them not being considerate or polite enough to merely providing a blanket because the patients would become anemic-like during the transfusions and get extremely cold. It wasn't like they were sick at that point. It was just a matter of the process you go through during dialysis.

At any rate, me and *"one"* of my lil' girlfriends were sitting at a red light in front of the mall, and what happens next?

BAM! That's all either of us remembered for a few minutes. Another car slammed into the back of her lil' brand new Ford Escort and knocked both our asses damn near through the dashboard and window.

By the time I came to, my dumb ass immediately leaped out the car whip lashed and all surging to the vehicle behind us, fixing to kick somebody's ass. Not because her car was fucked up but because now I really needed some dope. And these mothaphuckas don' fucked up my ride to get to it.

"Hey Deniece, you alright?"

She was crying and stiff, but said, "Yeah."

That was all I needed to know. Then I charged the guy walking towards me immediately. I started on his ass with what appeared to be about a thirty-piece. A thirty-piece on the streets is equivalent to hitting a person at least thirty times in a row before you finish him off. I mean, I attacked his ass like a swarm of bees. It took about eight onlookers to subdue me. Man, if he wasn't gon' take me to get my dope he deserved that ass whoopin'.

One problem though...*uh...it wasn't his car that hit us.* The car that rammed into us from the back had burnt the fuck off. They hit and run while Deniece and I were knocked out the few minutes after the impact. The gentleman whose ass I was whoopin' was an innocent onlooker who was pulling up to make sure we were okay and to impede the other oncoming traffic that was ensuing. Not only that, with my luck the police showed up.

We were waiting on the wreckers to show up, but until the police finished investigating the scene the wreck is secondary. They were trying to charge me with a brand new assault case, which had become the primary concern. Wasn't no easy way out of it. I didn't just hit the man a few times.

When they asked one of the witnesses how many times the man had been struck, she said, "Whew lawd, he hit that man about fawty times officer and very swiftly too, I might add."

Not good, that thirty-piece was now a forty-piece from a witness and at the wrong damn time, landing Eric's unlucky ass in the back seat of a police cruiser headed back downtown...*again*.

Obviously, I was in denial about that dope. Had to be. Couldn't have been the dominoes I was so anxious to get to.

Two funny things happened as I was being transported. First, the black cop was mocking the shit out of me saying, "Just like a dumb ass nigga to jump out the car after an accident that he wasn't the blame for and act a fool when his girlfriend had the best of Geico insurance available."

"Fuck you!" I yelled and I meant it, fuck him.

"Naw, fuck you! Jackass. 'Cause you the one fucked. You are the one who's on the way to jail because you was too stupid to play injured and not move out the front seat until the ambulance came. 'Cause your girlfriend 'bout to get paid."

Damn, I didn't let him know, but I did feel stupid. Nothing worse than being stupid and locked up. I think they go together anyway. Stupid and locked up...don't it? Well that was the first thing funny that happened.

The second thing funny was the wrecker driver apparently was a hustler. He towed my lil' 'sometime' girlfriend's car for free, or so she thought. Turned her on to a good doctor, lawyer and therapist. They were some kind of *hotshot wrecker-lawyer-chiropractor hustling ring*, apparently. Fine by me, especially since he also got an attorney to bail me out of jail and take on my case at the persistent request of my lil' 'sometime girlfriend' who I had no intention on making fulltime.

Not only that, she had the presence of mind to ask him what kind of qualifications did you need to become a wrecker driver. Apparently none, since they hired me immediately. Yeah, I got a *job* the day after I got out of jail. Never drove a wrecker before, but I learned. It was a piece of cake. I found out all the wrecker drivers were ex cons, including the guy that hired me. He was the biggest ex con. He needed someone to drive the extra wrecker truck he had. He also needed them to be green to the game and new, which he thought I was. He had life fucked up though. I may have been green to the wrecker game, but I wasn't green to game period. I quickly picked up on that hustle sport easily. Not soon enough obviously.

Initially, "they" got me the job. Her, being my 'lil' sometime girlfriend', so I could put something on them bills she accumulated while my *now* working ass was around there all day. Him, 'cause now there was a "Him" involved surprisingly. That was their setup. For me to be able to pay the attorney that got me out of jail, make him some money by driving his wrecker truck as an employee and making some extra money off me for having been green initially. All of this so my 'lil' sometime girlfriend' would cooperate with them and their lil' hustling scheme ensuring maximum return on her crying claim...only for her to end up his fulltime girlfriend. 'Cause eventually she started tripping and put me out. They had become an item, but they both had life fucked up. *They ain't gon' play me like that.*

So when I confronted the nigga, pistol cocked and everythang, he assured me that wasn't the route I wanted to take. Not if I wanted "HIS" attorney to beat that assault with bodily injury case. Adding, "And I am aware this would be your third strike."

I felt like all the air had been let out my balloon. There it was again. Some nigga done robbed me of something. Not only that, I had to work for him and watch the bitch end up pregnant in the next three months.

I confronted her. "I thought you couldn't have no more kids?!"

"A joke...you a mothaphuckin joke Eric Payson," my ex lil' sometime girlfriend had the nerve to say, crushing whatever sometime liking I had for her.

Grandmother said *"never let the joke be on you"* and what the fuck you go and do? The exact opposite. You ain't just the joke no more Eric...you are officially the butt of it.

CHAPTER 23

THAT'S WHAT SONS ARE FOR

Well, grandmother may have gotten it half right, but she wasn't completely right. Not yet anyway. She said don't *"end up"* being the butt of the joke. Actually I may have just started out looking like the joke, but I really liked this wrecker driver shit. And my, well their, attorney is really good too. He kept resetting the court date and he was already paid. I was able to pay him the entire twenty five hundred dollar retainer within a month of learning to drive the wrecker truck.

Man, I felt like I was balling a little. I was paying my bills. 'Cause I got me a fresh lil' one-bedroom loft apartment. Wasn't much, but it was enough for me. After three months, they let me break my lease to upgrade to a two bedroom. I didn't need it but I wanted it. One reason, I was so happy to be making some money I wanted to do something my mother and grandmother had always talked about aloud, like it was a fantasy for them. They both spoke of how glad they'd be when they were able to come to my house. Or at least say, *"I'm going over to my son's house for Thanksgiving."* My grandmother would say that to me and my brother also.

Derrick was selling dope now so nobody ever saw him that much anymore. He was staying with my grandmother for about three years, which gave me another reason not to go over there as much. Not much of a reason, I know. More like an excuse, huh?

I was really thinking it would give me some time to get my act together so she and I could be proud when I did come around. She always thought so much of me, irregardless of what I was going through, her and my mother. They both just knew it was some sort of test from God, especially for me.

I wasn't the least bit enthused about how special I was to God. I wanted to be regular. My grandmother thought I hardly ever visited like a grandson should, but the one hour or so I would take the time to stop by she still made me feel like that nine-year-old pissy lil' boy all over again. She always knew the truth without me telling it. My mother was pretty good at it too. She would say *"because I am your mother I know your heart son."*

That made it hard for me to lie to people that believed in me. So I would think I was being honorable by staying away until I was doing good, or right. Problem was, I seemed to never be doing good...for long.

But my brother, he didn't mind going around cause he wasn't afraid to do wrong or lie in their face. He was much wilder and daring than I when it came to grandmother.

At any rate, I was doing good now. *Might as well enjoy it, while it lasts.* And me not visiting mother while she was sick would always revisit me so I was eager to do something like a son for a change. I wanted to redeem myself to her and the family so I upgraded to the two bedroom. Just so I could decorate a room for mama. Yep, I was excited too.

Although I was calling more often, she didn't have a clue what I was doing. I was so excited that instead of starting to go visit her I decided I'd stay with my regular inconsistent routine so not to give it away.

I was dressing better, more clean cut and everything. Besides, I was working 10-to 12-hour shifts so I would be tired by the day's end. Not to mention working weekends and nights – the only thing I didn't like about the job. But it kept me out of trouble.

Anyway, I bought her a bedroom suit. It was solid gold...looking... you know what I mean...(shuddup). Brass, I think. Some shit mother would buy. Like her mother, everything had to be gold or have sequence in or on it. I got her a nice Jesus picture and frame. Then, all I needed to do was find the matching Martin Luther King picture to go with it. *Oh, it's just my mama, huh? Whatever...* eventually I found one. Well, it wasn't actually a picture but a fan. Laugh, if you want to, that was better than the picture 'cause she might think I'd been to church with that fan. Then again maybe not. That was a little far fetched.

I purchased a nice comforter. Not name brand or nothing, but it was nice to me. I got it from a garage sale (man, whateva! I'm trynna do something for my mama here...alright. Let a nigga make it, damn). Like I was saying, I got some of them lil' green plastic plants to make the room look livable and alive along with an alarm clock with the radio, some lil' ornaments and accessories to go on the dresser and a big Valentine teddy bear. Even though it was June, I couldn't pass up on the deal. The lady was trying to get rid of everything at the garage sale. And the Valentine bear in June was included.

I was a decorating mothaphucka jack. All I wanted was for my mother to say, "I'm going over to my son's house this weekend.

I didn't need a car because the wrecker truck was my transportation. She could get transported to dialysis in a wrecker truck couldn't she? At that time, it didn't matter because she was. If I knew my mother, she would rather ride with me in the company vehicle so she could tell somebody her son was working. Let her tell it, *"He's the manager."*

My grandmother would often make mention of that too saying, "Eric you could do anything you wanted to, you that smart boy. You could be the manager of a Jack-in-the-Box in a month if you would just go."

Shiiiit, little did she know, I wasn't going to work at no damn Jack in the Box, but maybe she did know. At any rate, it took me all of about five months to get everything bought, paid for and situated. Me and mother were talking pretty often via phone.

This day, she said something to me – something that made me feel like I was suffocating. She had been on dialysis for a while, and her heart was in bad condition as a result so she was unable to receive her kidney transplant. She had been dieting for a while so she could get healthy enough to get her kidney. My mother was a devout Christian at that point and her faith was her rock. She just always knew God was gonna see to it that she got her kidney.

It didn't help with mama losing friends to the very disease she was battling. There were these ladies, friends of hers that she made unbeknownst to us. These were people my mother had grown fond of while defending them at the dialysis center, without their permission or consent. Some were much younger than her, but they started dying off one by one.

My mother was a very strong willed, determined, fearless and brave lady, as you can tell by now so it shook my whole world up to hear her say this to me, "Eric they say yo' mama need a kidney real bad and I don't want to ask you or your sister. Your sister because she now has a family...and well...I know you probably would do it..."

PROBABLY!? Man, this was better than all that Thanksgiving dinner shit and apartment living and coming to visit stuff. This would be my *redemption*. I could finally prove my love to my mother like everyone doubted. The more I internalized it, the more eager I got. That excitement was soon nullified when she looked at me with a fear I never seen my lil' brave mother possessed with and added, "I'm getting scared baby."

All the blood stopped circulating through my veins. My body tightened up and a lump began to swell and lodge in my throat. My nerves started to wither as my lungs filled up with air ready to explode. I was desperately trying to think of something consoling to say, but my brain wouldn't process any information. And even if it could, my mouth wouldn't allow me to speak. My tongue was stuck to the roof of my mouth. All I saw was my mama out of all the mama's in the world was facing me and breathing her fear into my lungs, into my veins, into my blood, piercing my very soul...to death. It was a matter of minutes before I could finally muster the strength to barely utter with tears patiently waiting near the ducts of my eyes, "You ain't got to be scared mama."

I took her by the hand, nestling her weary head onto my chest. Looking to the sky, I told her, "That's what sons are for mama. We gon' be alright...we gon' be alright."

CHAPTER 24

NEVER FELT THAT KIND OF FEAR

I ain't never felt so helpless and vulnerable in all my life. I couldn't imagine that kind of torment. Everyday, every hour, every minute of the rest of what life you may or may not have left, petrified that your last breath may very well be your last breath. I merely couldn't "imagine" that kind of torment. But when the person that is being helplessly petrified with that kind of torment and fear is that close and that special to you that makes your agony double.

This wasn't just a special person. It was my special mama! Say that with me...my mama man! You feel what I'm saying?

The *only* one you are given. The *only* one you gon' get and the *only* one you gon' ever have. It don't get no special than that. You can have four or five daddies, step-mama, Godmother, wives and girlfriends and what not. But nothing ever gon' top or match a mama to a boy. The closest it gets to that is a grandmother. The first thing you see a young man say on TV when he gets his fifteen minutes of fame is *"Hi Mom!"* It didn't matter if he ain't never met her and his daddy raised him all his life and it didn't matter if his stepmother raised him and he knew she loved him and he loved her. He still would *say* "Hi Mom!" Not "Hi Daddy" and damn sho' not "Hi Step-Mom."

So now I'm scared for her and they cant get this kidney fast enough. One problem, they have to do lots of tests on you and your blood. One to make sure you are compatible and second to check any ailments you may have. Mind you, I ain't ever had no insurance and me and my potnas all have been to the doctor for penicillin...mm-mm. Products of the irresponsible lifestyle a nigga was living.

Let's just say we have a street rule that you ain't ever out the woods, even when you do stop doing irresponsible shit. See something 'bout irresponsible and careless behavior. It can show up when it want to or even worse, *when you least expect it.* In other words, anytime.

Well, this ain't the time to be finding out you HIV positive or got cancer of anything, especially when yo' mama's life is depending on it. Under any other circumstance, a nigga wouldn't want to know that status, but my mama and my redemption were at stake. Wasn't nothing gon' make her think I thought twice about me saving her life. Not this time and after it being said I was the one killing her.

Lord say the same, she gon' get this kidney. Both of them if she need 'em. Hell I'd rather be on dialysis instead.

Then I got good news and I got bad news, if you can understand that. (Which one you want first?)

Let's go with the good news. We were compatible and I wasn't HIV, HPV or any other Q, R, S, T, U, V. However, the bad news was mama would have to have surgery again and because her body was so susceptible to any and every infection she couldn't stay well long enough for them to prep for a surgery. Every doctor she went to couldn't figure out what was going on with her immune system. Until she went to this specialist and he diagnosed it as a *thyroid condition* and told her it needed to be removed. That went as planned, so good news again.

Three weeks after surgery, they decided to give mama one of my kidneys. I was too have the operation in a month. I was gon' get my redemption. "Hi Mom!" I was gon' get to say it too. "Hi Mom."

I was so eager to have the surgery done to give life back to my mother.

She still hadn't seen her room in the apartment. I decided I'd wait until after the surgery to surprise her. Then the bad news happened. Unfortunately a lil' fifteen-year-old was killed in a car accident in New Orleans. Anytime somebody was killed it was the sad news, I guess. But this was worse.

Mama called me at 5 a.m. that morning crying hysterically, "Eric! Eric! I might have a kidney."

I said, "I know mama. We already discussed this, I thought."

She replied, "No baby, you might not have to give me yours. A lil' girl was killed in an accident and my name came up on the donor list."

I initially got upset for the doctors even saying some shit like that. For one, they had gotten her excited before about this and she ended up disappointed that it never materialized. And for two, she had a kidney already...MINE! I didn't think much of it when we got off the phone, other than *I wish I had that doctor's number. I'd cuss his ass out, and yeah I said cuss.* "Why they fuckin" with her emotions like that?"

It wasn't 45 minutes before the phone rang again and woke me up out my semi sleep, again.

"Eric! Eric! I got my kidney. I got my kidney! They flying it in now. I'm on my way to the hospital now. Y'all come on."

That was supposed to be good news to me, but instead of being happy I was sad, hurt and disappointed. Somebody had robbed me of my glory again. For a change, I needed to give my mama something nobody else could. I sat on the edge of that bed for an entire hour crying. This wasn't just about a kidney for me. Nobody would ever understand this was about redemption. A son's redemption. That would be the step to catapult me into manhood. And all it took was the kidney of a fifteen-year-old stranger to remind me of how much of a boy I was...and probably was always gon' be. My life depended on this moment, but right now all I wanna do is die to keep me from killing myself.

CHAPTER 25

WHO GON' SEE THE GOOD

Mama's surgery went well. When she got out, the first person she looked for and spoke to was me. "Eric, Eric... they said I did good Eric," she mustered right before she drifted back off into her coma-like sleep.

I was careful not to make any noise or disturb her while she rested, given the doctors said she wasn't out of the woods yet. The kidney could still reject. I was overwhelmed that her mind and heart were preoccupied with me during her time of need. I immediately left the room so she wouldn't worry about me, walking briskly up the hallway, down the stairs and down the street with my head down.

After walking quite a ways down, I noticed my brother in law "B.L." had been following me from a distance, just to keep an eye on me I assumed. Never saying a word. His way of saying he understood my pain, grief and guilt, and that I wasn't alone.

"I know you love your mama," he said when he caught up to me.

It was refreshing to know or think someone understood without me having to explain it. It felt good to know he cared, which made me want to give my family a reason to.

Mama slept for a couple of days straight, in and out, it seemed. I had almost forgotten about my court date that was coming up in the next couple of days. I was gon' try and play it by ear and wait until mama was at least out of the hospital, but no one knew exactly when that would or could be. They seemed to be running tests every and all day, a very tedious process we came to find out. Given her immune system was almost brand new like a baby and shut down, mama was even more susceptible to infections and at that time infections could be fatal. Though everybody was happy, I was still emotionless and paying attention to everything. Something just wouldn't let me get excited... my guilt.

I just didn't want my mama to wake up again in a hospital and I not be right there when she was to lay eyes on me. On that note, I didn't worry about that court date from the altercation I got into during the car accident and it was a good thing I didn't 'cause mama was in the hospital for a whole month. This time, I stayed the whole time knowing there was an arrest warrant waiting for me. Who knew what that meant? I didn't dare reveal that to anyone. But bad went to worse when my job started harassing me about the time I'd taken off.

I told my boss, "Mothaphucka do you understand my mama could be on her death bed! Cars gon' still need towing when I get back. Y'all better wait," and I was dead serious.

I guess they were too. 'Cause upon my return I realized they came and picked up the truck from my apartment. *Now, I don' lost my job...I guess.*

Plus, I had a big bright red notice on my door that from the looks of it had been there for a week or so, along with an eviction notice. My lights were to be turned off that evening, and I was to be out of the apartment by the end of next week. Aw shit! Had I had my job, I could have borrowed the money and let them take it out of my check.

*That's okay. I'll go to another wrecker company...*but in and with what?! I totally forgot the only transportation I had was that wrecker truck. And now I'm tapped out of money without even enough for bus fare. I had to do something and in a hurry, so I went to this old piggy bank I kept a few quarters in and scrounged enough of them together to get my fare to a wrecker company on the other side of town.

I was desperate, I needed that job to keep up my newfound status I had become accustomed to. Plus, I needed to get back and forth out of town to see my mother. She was used to me coming and needed me now. I had to complete what I started. I couldn't let her down now, nor myself. My life was still depending on this redemption of sorts. I got to get it right I would repeat to myself... no excuses.

It was just my luck they were in need of two drivers immediately starting that day. Man that was a relief.

I think I'll start going to church after this one. I'm getting some good blessings, just like mama said I would.

After riding that bus all day, all the way from one side of town to the other and about three transfers in the process, I had to catch them again immediately before the close of business day downtown if I wanted to take possession of the truck that day and start working. Not only did I need to start working but I needed to ask for an advance. Remember my utilities were 'bout to be terminated and I had an eviction notice.

I catch the two buses needed to get downtown and it's about 3:30 when I get Downtown to the Tows' driver's license office. They closed at 4 p.m. I was hoping they processed my information because it was Friday too. People wanted to get off and get their weekend started so they had a tendency to work slow and ineffectively on Friday afternoons.

Out of the five ladies left in the office, one stayed late each day just for instances like this. She didn't get off 'til 5 p.m. Yippee! Saved. My life was saved. She probably thought I had a mental problem the way I was thanking her repeatedly. "Ooh thank you ma'am! Whew wee you just don't know what this means ma'am. I shol' does thanks ya ma'am." I was sounding that desperate, like a runaway slave being hid from his captors. She might have felt sorry for me, which might explain the solemn look on her face. It didn't matter, I was grateful. She didn't know my testimony.

As she was processing everything down, I began to tell her my story. Didn't seem like she was listening, but I was eager and excited to continue fixing up my mama's bedroom. I needed desperately for her to see what I had been doing since she recovered.

It was about six o'clock once I got through with fingerprint and that was gon' be the first driver's license picture I was gon' smile on. When I saw the camera, I thought, *Ya' know, maybe I outta smile more often.*

I sat down and waited on my license. *Back to work Jack! Can't keep a good man down. I'm Eric Payson. Eric Payson damn it,* is all I was thinking.

"Eric Payson!" someone said aggressively snapping me out of my back-to-work euphoria. I looked toward the doorway. "You will need to come with us."

I stood up and one of the officers turned me around, frisked me, and proceeded to put me in handcuffs. "What's going on?", I asked, as the officer interrupted.

"You have a warrant for your arrest for assault with bodily injury and. Also for failure to comply with the courts."

Motha-phuck-a! OH MY GOD! NOOOOOOOO!!! As I looked back at the lady that had been processing my information, I felt mortified and betrayed. She wouldn't even look up at me. She didn't have the nerve. All the time she knew...she knew. That's why she wasn't responding or answering my pleas, not looking at me. I totally forgot under all of my duress that I had missed that court date while visiting mama.

Even worse, it was the weekend and ain't no judge available 'til Monday. I was sick to my stomach. Everything was riding on this accomplishment and yet again I don' fucked it off. I was speechless, exhausted and disgusted. I guess you *can* keep a good man down, if he ever can become one. But until then...you just keep his good ass locked up, until he decide to become a man. But who gon' see the good in that man at all after that though?

...mama's

CHAPTER 26

REDEMPTION TIME

That weekend, I was in a complete panic in that jail cell. I don't know why when I had been there plenty of times before. But not when I had a plan to get my shit together. This was the last thing I needed for my mama to find out, not while she was on her sick bed. So I had to do something that I hated to have to do. Call the one and only person besides my mama or sister who wouldn't hesitate to bail me out of a situation like this. I especially hated to do it while I was attempting to be responsible.

I didn't call on this person unless it was life and death, which in this situation it was. And that person was someone my mama had been beggin' me to get with and keep in touch with for the past five to ten years. I was, I mean, I planned on it, but like I said this person could tell when I wasn't doing right, even when I hadn't revealed it to them. It was so hard to lie to them, it seemed, 'til I just stayed away when I wasn't doing anything respectable to keep from attempting to lie. I just wanted to have something good to say whenever they had to lay eyes on me. Besides this was the lady who got me out of jail whenever I found myself in there. Whether I had been around or not. My daddy's mama would come to my rescue, just as she had done for him and my grandfather – Mama Dorothy, my grandmother. She didn't like none of her boys *sitting* in no white man's jail. Evidently her boys didn't get that memo.

It was rumored that the bank put up the money for a 60,000-dollar bond for my grandfather when he was incarcerated for some warehouse filled with stolen weapons and goods. That's how good the Godfather's credit was.

Undoubtedly, I would have to wait until Monday to make the call. I wasn't sure what the status with my apartment or my job would be at that point.

Finally, Monday came and I went before the judge to enter my plea. I entered a plea of not guilty figuring after I get some doctors and hospital info to the courts that would suffice. If worse could get worse, as it usually did for me, I found out I wouldn't get a trial for another week.

Oh, no, I knew I'd don' lost the job now, unless I could get out of there. I was desperate once again, so I had no choice but to call Mama Dorothy.

To no avail, I made the collect call eight times in a row. Given that my grandmother was always at the house, her not answering the phone was baffling. I tried again later that night, knowing she couldn't see and didn't drive at night. Eight to ten more times and no answer.

Maybe it's one of the study nights at the church, I thought. I told you, she was always at church at some kind of study...bible study, Baptist Training Reunion...Study, Mission Study, Usher Board #1, #2 and #3...Study. Church was always studying is all I knew. And my grandmother was gon' be studying with them.

Tuesday, I frantically attempted to reach her to the point that I phone checked niggas about the phone. I was extremely paranoid.

Hopefully, no one was missing me yet or looking for me. Good thing, if it can be considered a good thing, I often came up missing in action for periods at a time.

After a week I was really concerned about my grandmother not answering her phone, fearing the worst.

I found out I violated my probation, which I had one month left of. The judge was willing to release me on the contingency I had a job and a place of residency for at least six months, which I had. So I was elated that I would be released. When they called me back up for verification and to let me know, they could *not* verify any of the references, or residency. I had indeed lost my new job before I even started and my apartment. The last month of my probation would be served incarcerated. Or maybe it would be the last month of my life. If not my life, then someone close to me. I could feel it.

My family was concerned and had been looking to get in touch with me. They knew just where to look...the county jail. A week after learning my fate, I got the news that my mother indeed had passed away from congestive heart failure.

The judge wouldn't allow a temporary release for me to attend the services because I had a few incidents involving evading arrest and some other priors. I should've been more careful of what I wish for. I said I hated to see my mother sick and planned not to attend the services if it ever happened. Well, that was when I was totally selfish and irresponsible. I am not anymore and God knew it, so why? I also remembered mama 'nem saying, 'sometime what you do in your past, has a way of showing up in your future at the most inopportune times.' That God knew too and now so do I. I had to miss my mama's home going.

I missed her waking up to me after the completion of her surgery. I missed her seeing her bedroom I had been working on diligently. I missed her suffering in the hospital with the opportunity to put that last smile on her face. I missed my chance at redemption when the opportunity came for me to give her a kidney. I missed being a son for all of those years she was here, and especially while she was sick. And now I missed the last chance to see my mother in person, dead or alive. My mind froze and my chest felt like it was compressed under two hundred thousand tons of pressure.

The voices in my head were at maximum octave, on permanent scream. I spiraled and spider webbed quietly out of control. I couldn't unball my fists or stop the surging and urging of power surmounting and building up in my veins, Attempting to release the pressure through my nerves so I could breathe, I weep "MAMAAAAAAAAAAAAAAAAAAAAAAAAAAAAAAA!!!!!!!"

...

...

...

In my head I was screaming, but it wouldn't come out of my mouth. I needed to unleash the cry sooo bad, but I couldn't. After all, I was in jail. There was no corner for crying in there... no crier's corner, what the hell kind of place is that for a human? And being that I couldn't cry, I wanted to kill something or go somewhere and die myself.

I had nothing else to live for at that point and no reason to ask *why.*

CHAPTER 27

THE LETTER FROM MAMA

I spent the last month in jail quiet and to myself, contemplating suicides, homicides, genocides and whatever other sides that could go with that 3 piece. I never seen that one coming. But maybe I did. However I never expected that I would be that irresponsible to the point that even when I was being responsible it would be too late. *"See just 'cause you start to do right...don't mean life forgets what you done wrong"* was one of mama's favorite quotes. Mama's last days were spent without me, her one only son by her side holding her hand. The one side amongst all those others I had been contemplating.

Come to find out, my family tried desperately to get me out the county. Every measure within reason was taken without misrepresenting mama. They even held the body seventeen days in their attempt, seventeen days!!

Mama had everything already planned and figured out, like she usually did . The casket color, dress she wanted, the songs, choir, the solo songstress and the pastor she wanted to eulogize her. Not to mention, she had chosen the funeral home and cemetery plot.

The day of my release my sister had the pictures ready for me to view in the car while she drove straight to the cemetery to allow me time to eulogize mama...in and at peace finally. At first, it was excruciatingly painful to stand on the ground that my mother was buried underneath. I could feel my mother's spirit around me. I imagined sanking into that sand, and back into my mama in which I had come from. I wanted to resurrect her from the ground and make her rise up like the Jesus she so faithfully believed in. I wanted my mama back, just to see and look at her one more time at least, pleeease Lord!. Sensing this was a good time for me to hear from mama, my sister handed me a note from her.

Eric my one and only son. I am sorry for the anguish and any pain I may have caused you my son. Mama only knew what mama knew at the time, but please know mama only wanted better for you and your sister so you didn't have to go through what I had to. I ask that you forgive me for any role I have played in any part of your not becoming successful in life...yet. Because I know you will. I ask you to forgive me just as I had to forgive my mama for only knowing what she knew at the time son. And I ask that when you do have kids you do better by them also. The best you know how to see that they don't have to go through what mama and Eric did. That's all we can do son, is our best. God will give you credit for effort and God will handle the rest son.. I know you don't like to go to church, but God is real son. And God is good, Eric. The sooner you realize that baby, the sooner you gon be cleared of all your troubles and all your demons. I'll be so glad when you give your life to God. I prayed and prayed and prayed and prayed I'd live to see it. But mama was getting tired son. It's not your fault so don't you go being hard on yourself. I know without a doubt it is going to happen for you! because I am your mother and you are my one and only son Eric Jerome Payson. I know your heart son and God knows it too. God watches over children and fools Eric (smiling).Mama know you ain't know fool, but I ask God to continue watching over you until your dying day son. Yo' mama and God tight like that, he'll do it for your mama (winks). I knew I may not live to see it Eric.. Mama's was just tired baby...

I often look forward to going home to be with my Jesus and the rest of my family that's gone home. Especially your daddy. I want to see your daddy in person again, cleansed with the water he's been drinking from the fountain of Heaven

If mama's not around to see you when you give yourself to God, you open this note and know it ain't nothing you did you got to be ashamed of with me. I know why you wasn't at the hospital better than you know yourself. You not selfish or hateful. I know you was scared baby and ashamed. You wanted to be the one to save your mama. You wanted to help me Eric. Now mama's not here for you to worry about. But you still can help yourself son. Start going to church, and reading your Bible everyday Eric, to get the word of the Lord in your blood.

And go by and spend some time with your grandmother more, Eric. She is getting older now and we ain't always promised to be here. All she got is you and Derrick. Please do that for me and don't wait 'til it's too late... like I know you will do. I say that 'cause if I don't it will drive me crazy up here in Heaven. And I ain't going to be acting crazy up here. I plan on doing just as the song says "walking around all day... In heaven." Get right with God. Get right with your grandmother. Get right with your life and get right with yourself son And I know you and your sister are going to always look out for one another. I ask this a many other blessings, in Jesus name... Amen. I love you son.

Your Loving Mother,

Aubrey Ida-Marie Payson

P.S. I'm still holding on to your hand son.

Holding on to the tear-soaked letter, I got so weak that I fell to my knees sobbing like a baby. I couldn't stop myself from crying. Was this why I was being tortured? Because I wasn't right with God or my grandmother, yet?

My sister allowed me some time to grieve, as she cried profusely knowing she had yet another blow to deliver to me.

Teary eyed, Bay Bay said, "Eric, this gon' seem like it has gotten worse, and I hate to tell you this now. But you have to make it better this time around. You gon' have to be strong man! Mama Dorothy had a stroke too...a severe one Eric." She paused and then continued, "'You have to be there for her."

"What!?" I rose to my feet, suddenly.

"She had a stroke a few weeks ago. She doesn't even know

mama's dead. She don't recognize nobody anymore, but she keeps mumbling for you and Derrick."

Somehow, the tears just evaporated and I was up on my feet, mind moving a mile a minute.

"What hospital is she in and have y'all talked to Derrick?"

"Yes but he was too distraught. He didn't want to hear anymore. You know he lives in California now and said he wanted to wait and talk to you before he made a decision on traveling. I got his number."

Hurrying to the car I told Bay- Bay, "Call him up right now!"

She handed me her phone and I dialed his number several times without an answer, so I was forced to leave a message. As we were driving to the hospital, I couldn't help but keep looking at mama's pictures in that casket. As paranoid as I was all my life about that eerie spirit of death, caskets and funeral homes, this time it had a calming affect. I think those pictures of mama in that casket helped me this time. They spoke to me. She was in fact helping me and holding my hand. Guiding me just as she said she would in the letter. Just as she said she would in life.

I was shocked that Mama Dorothy could even take sick. She was supposed to be invincible, at least that's what we thought. I had no idea what I was about to witness until I went into that hospital room with all of them church folks and new cousins I ain't never met before.

The people barely spoke to me and I overheard one of them say "that's one of 'em."

Another whispered, "Where he been?"

And yet another answered loud enough to be heard, "In jail 'prolly, where they always at." At times, church people can be so messy to be so Godly.

They weren't even trying to whisper, so my arrogance took over and I didn't speak to either of them. This time instead of getting shame, I became ornery...like I could be at times. This was still my grandmother and wasn't nothing but blood gon' change that.

Unlike with mama, I was gon' be there. I wasn't leaving her side and when she woke up good she was gon' see her grandson right there...at her side. I didn't have any warrants and I didn't have nowhere to go. All the more reason for me to stay right there.

I did see one familiar face seated in the corner of the hospital room. A big burly looking fella, clean cut with glasses, a snow-white beard and mini white semi-afro.

When he reached out his hand to shake mine, he said, "You prolly don't 'memba me. Me and ya granddaddy was good friends. I'm Bobby." Still locked in a firm handshake I looked puzzled, so he added, "You might know me as Humphrey."

"OH yeah! Humphrey" Why was Humphrey here?

I immediately got excited though, especially when he added, "Don't worry about the usher board. They up here being nosey asking about business that don't pertain to them."

"Like what," I asked.

"Insurance policies and whatnots."

"Insurance policy? She just had a stroke, she ain't dead." I could feel the fury mounting up. Usher board or not, wasn't nobody messing over my grandmother.

Humphrey nodded his head toward the door and started walking out into the hallway. I followed him.

"That's what we needed to tell you. Well, I wanted to tell you and your brother together. Do you know when he will get here?"

"No, I been trying to get in touch with him though."

Humphrey said, "If it's alright with you, I much rather speak with both of you together."

I didn't think nothing of it, so I agreed. It never dawned on me that Mama Dorothy in the hospital was anything more than temporary. Upon returning to the hospital room, I noticed some of the usher board members had gathered around her bed. Grandma had began to awake.

I sat back trying to keep from being an asshole from the looks and stares they gave me when I arrived.

I heard my sister say, *"he's right here Mama Dorothy."* Bay-Bay motioned her finger summoning me to come closer to the bed.

I didn't mind being in the room, but I didn't like seeing her sick like that, even though she just looked like she was awakening from a nap. It was all of the funeral arrangements and grim aura in the room that got to me. Just as it was at her house that I hated to visit since I was a little boy. Flowers and cards with Jesus' picture on 'em everywhere. It seemed like it could be Heaven, or maybe I wouldn't know the difference. Or just maybe I wouldn't be so paranoid if I wasn't so used to hell.

As I walked to her, her eyes opened wide and lit up as they hurried past all those usher board #2 on lookers trying to get her attention. She reached and grabbed my hand and squeezed it hard as she could and looked at me with that big ole wide rule gate-mouf smile. The one that I inherited from her. The one that could light up a thousand Christmas trees. She uttered them famous words she always said when she hadn't seen me in a long time and was happy to see me, "Good God almighty boy!"

"Hey mama," I said and then leaned down close to her ear. Amongst all the nosiness surrounding us, I whispered, "How you feeling?"

She replied sternly, "How you feeling?"

I was amazed. She was still the same lil' feisty, cool, quick-witted lady she'd always been.

"I'm alright," I said.

She then said, "Well, I'm alright then," and gave me that big gate-mouf mile wide grin again. She then said, "As long as I got you, I'm gon' be alright now. Now find yo' brother and get him here, so we all can be alright."

"Yes ma'am, yes ma'am."

That was all I needed to know was that she needed me there and it made things better as opposed to worse. I wasn't leaving for sure now.

That also made the church ladies ease up on me a lil'. Funny how they all started acting like they remembered me, suddenly. Rubbin' and lustin' on me like I was a piece of porn and they were the perverts. Just nosey, asking all kinds of questions they didn't have no business asking still. Like nosey wasn't even a word to them...no shame at all.

All except for two ladies that came that I had much respect for, Ms. Lucinda and Ruby Jean. They were two ladies that were always spoken highly of by my grandmother. And though she was very much a loner, these were two of the few people she would spend time away from home with such as during Thanksgiving dinners, and things of that nature.

When they walked in, the place came into some good energy. They and I both made a mad beeline toward each other and greeted each other with hugs and well wishes. I was so glad to see some faces from the church I was familiar with. Ruby Jean told me that she had gotten in touch with Derrick and his plane would be there tonight.

My grandmother didn't appear sick at all. She sat up cracking inside church jokes with the numerous visitors that were coming to and from. None of their jokes were funny, but all of hers were.

Nightfall came and everyone wanted to see my brother, including me who hadn't seen him in years. Mama Dorothy was resting and I wondered if she even knew I was there. I couldn't wait for her to go home from that place, so I could let her know I would nurse her back to health like a grandson should. The phone rang and I hurried to answer it before it disturbed her rest.

"How is she?" It was Derrick. Come to find out he was just like me in this department. He was terrified of hospitals and anybody in them.

"She's fine man," I said. "She just wants you here."

Impatient, he replied, "I'm on my way up there my nigga."

I laughed because my lil' brother had G-d up on me. I said, "Alright *nigga*, I'm here dawg," and hung up.

A few minutes later, Derrick peeked around the door and then walked in. I just started laughing again as I got up to hug my younger but gangster like brother. "Come in man. She's sleep."

We hugged, high-fived and exchanged daps. Grandmamma must've been able to smell us both because though we weren't loud she knew her only two offspring to her one and only son were finally there with her, together as she requested.

She said, "Eric, is that Derrick?"

"Yes ma'am," we both said simultaneously as we went to opposite sides of her bed.

She weakly grabbed both our hands and held them tightly... pulled us in close and tight and just looked at us with a long stare before she smiled with that gate-mouf wide smile. I couldn't help but smile back. I loved to see that smile because it reminded me so much of me and where I came from.

On the other hand, Derrick just stared at her and started weeping. Nothing else needed to be said...nothing. It was a wrap. I knew just like she said it would. Get your brother here so everything would be alright. At that very moment, no one could tell me different.

CHAPTER 28

I GOT YO' HOSPICE

Mama Dorothy finally had both of her boys at her side. That was all she wanted and all she needed for things to get better, at least that's how it appeared. She didn't want the church , no strangers or bystanders taking care of her. She wanted her own family, her immediate family, her only family – her one and only dead son's two offspring and we were eager to step up to the plate, finally.

As luck would have it, got a call at my sister's house about the wrecker job I didn't get because I missed my court date. It was a good thing that I used the correct references on the application this time. I usually didn't because somebody was always looking for me. However, the wrecker company wanted me to start work immediately, from 6 p.m. to 6 a.m. Now that Derrick was in town that would work out perfectly. I didn't have anyplace to go anyway, so I could wash up at the hospital in the morning and be there to assist mama too. Kill two birds with one stone.

So Derrick and I worked out a schedule. Between the two of us, he would be there at night while I was at work and I would stay during the day.

"Man, I think I'm gon' stay at the house during the day then. Try to get me some shut eye 'cause these hospital sofas be fuckin' my back up," Derrick said.

I didn't think anything of it. I was cool with it. I knew who wasn't gonna be staying there at the house day or night...Eric. Because I still hated that house, or at least hated to spend the night in it. It still made me uneasy after all these years. It was old too so the building spoke to you at night. The foundation would be shifting and stuff too much. I guess I could have gotten cool with it or outgrew it, but hell it never spoke in the daytime. It only became creepy and cemetery-like at night. At any rate I ain't trusting the Amity in that Ville.

Once we got our schedules tight, Derrick immediately contacted Humphrey. I was surprised he knew him or knew to call him and wondered why he was even calling Humphrey at all. I finally asked him after he told me Humphrey was downstairs and on his way up here to have a talk with the both of us.

"That talk, the one that Humphrey told me he wanted to wait and have with me when Derrick was there?", I thought aloud.

Derrick filled me in on the details a bit. What he told me shook me to the core. Our grandmother wasn't coming home this time supposedly. The unit we were on was in fact the *hospice* part of St. Joseph's Hospital. Humphrey was her power of attorney and executer of the estate and he would come up to brief us on some things *when* Mama Dorothy dies.

"Dies! What? Dies? When she dies? She didn't appear nothing like DIES to me. Her spirit was excellent. She just sleepin' a lot Derrick...Not DIES," I pleaded in disbelief.

He said, "Naw Big Bro, that's why I flew on down here. When I talked to Humphrey, he told me it wasn't looking good and to get here as soon as I could."

That shit went right over my head. I didn't, wouldn't, and couldn't comprehend none of that dies bullshit. It wasn't gon' be no dying. Not on my watch. Not by my grandmother. I quickly became suspect a lil'. I wondered why did Humphrey tell me he would wait 'til Derrick came before he would disclose anything, but go ahead and discuss it with him anyway. So I asked Derrick.

"Why did Humphrey tell you the news, but when I talked to him he said he wanted to wait until the both of us were together to discuss it?"

Of course, Derrick had the perfect answer. "Say man, he cool."

Come to find out Derrick knew Humphrey pretty good from back in the day when he was living with grandmother and selling dope out her house, all in that lil' serene neighborhood. Derrick had that lil' serene corner of that lil serene street lit up, or so I heard.

"Humphrey never stopped coming by to visit after granddaddy got killed," Derrick said. "He would always check in on Mama Dorothy and he just never stopped. He also turned me on to my hook up. You know him and Big Al was connected. I had to take advantage of that Big Bro."

I had no idea or clue but it was understandable, since I myself hadn't been around like I should have. I didn't think to look into the situation. If my brother vouched for him, it was cool with me. It also made me admire him more, being he would look out for her like that and his good buddy....my grandfather.

I still wasn't completely sold on this hospice thing. Why? All I knew was I wasn't thinking about my grandmother's death at a time like this or anything that went with it. My mother had just died, I couldn't take another death so soon. I didn't want anything she was gon' leave behind to us either. I wanted her to stay here and live with us, like I would have wanted someone to be hoping, wishing and praying for me.

Well, no sooner than Derrick vouched for Humphrey...no sooner than he had turned on him. Because like I said, when Humphrey finally did come up to explain all that executor and hospice stuff I wouldn't even entertain the idea. So he and Derrick went in there to sign the papers with the doctors and doors closed. I don't know what went on behind those shut doors and didn't care as long as it had something to do with that dies campaign. Eric was not co-signing on that one. Mama Dorothy wasn't gon' ever live to see my name was on no shit counting her out the game, already. I knew she was gon' live.

See for one thing, I still wasn't getting that hospice shit. That's where they take you to die, apparently. This is the place that makes going out easy and nice, peaceful-like. Well, no I didn't understand hospice yet and what part of me hospice didn't understand...*that* I didn't understand. Nor did I care. I could give a shit what hospice stood for. All I knew was what *grandson* stood for. *This* grandson at that. *This* grandson was standing for life with his grandmother and not falling for hospice, hospital or hot sauce.

That was what was going on in my head so as you can see I was in denial. This shit was not registering. I was unable to make sense of any of it, initially. Remember, I was still very much irresponsible and irrational. However, in this case those traits were working for me, not against me.

It all started to make sense once Humphrey and Derrick went downstairs to smoke a cigarette and a mini argument or disagreement occurred, I guess. Derrick came back upstairs looking tight in the face.

"What's wrong?" I asked him. He nodded his head toward the hallway, not wanting to talk over mama. As I walked by her bed, it dawned on me that she had been sleeping for a while now.

Blowing off some steam, Derrick sighed and said, "*Humphrey was not able to give me the key to the house because no one can go into the house until after the will was read.*"

"Will for what? She ain't dead!" I was still in denial. I assume they were thinking *she ain't dead...yet,* but it didn't matter one way or the other to me 'cause she wasn't dead. I couldn't conceive her dying and I wasn't the one wanting to go to or trying to stay at that house anyway. I would just wait until she got discharged home.

When I replied, "But Derrick, I thought you said he was cool," he went into a rant about how crooked the nigga was and how we better watch him. I was really thinking, *It's too late for that. We should have been watching out for our own grandmother and he wouldn't have had to.* I didn't say that to my erratic brother though, but it's what ran across my mind.

I figured being they knew each other things would work themselves out.

Later that evening, we did as planned. I went to work and stopped by the hospital a few times to check on mama and Derrick, given I worked in that downtown zone now. I noticed she was up and awake but looking off in space like she was seeing illusions. Derrick was on the sofa sleeping and snoring like a pig.

Mama Dorothy began to knot herself up in fetal position like something was cornering her. I don't know what made me watch this for a second before I yelled out to her, but she was looking up, balling her body up like she was in fear.

Suddenly she started screaming out, "Nooo! Nooo! Nooo! Button, not Button!"

As Derrick jumped up, I went to her side. I shook her and said, "Mama, what's wrong?"

When she snapped out of it and regained her right state of mind, she unveiled that big gate-mouf wide smile again. This time it wasn't so soothing.

For the first time, I sensed the sickness and illness that was consuming her mind and body. Fortunately, it didn't have complete control of her spirit yet, nor did it have complete control of mine. And I wasn't about to let it get the best of me...or her.

I stroked my hand through her salt-n-pepper mini - fro, when she said she was thirsty. It was then that I realized that I had been there for two days and hadn't seen her eat or drink anything. I somehow felt responsible for that. Then, I noticed it wasn't one of them hospital jugs in the room either, nothing to pour water out of...no because this ain't the hospital no more Eric Payson. This _hospice_, not hospital.

Come to find out in hospice they don't feed or drink you either. They are there to make you comfortable. I'm still trying to figure out how you gon' be comfortable with no food or drank. Anyway, I'm in denial about this and ain't shit changed. All of this trying to make shit comfortable is making me _un_comfortable.

I went to the nurses' station to complain a bit and complain I did because I didn't like the answers I was getting from the nurse that responded to the buzzer. She was feisty too. _Aint supposed to be no feisty in the hospital...let alone in the hospice, I thought.._

They're supposed to be peaceful, I knew that much, but this bitch had an attitude...a _bad_ attitude.

With an irritable look on her face the nurse suggested, "Mr. Payson, because of the nature of your grandmother's illness, which was a stroke, she isn't supposed to eat or drink anything. The only nutrients she will get will be intravenously. The reason for this is she could choke or suffocate to death because her esophagus is very weak."

I went off then. "I be damn if I'm gon' be in here and let my grandmother say she thirsty and she not get a drink of water!"

The nurses started moving around there like chickens with their heads cut off 'cause I was gon' wake every half dead mothaphucka up and getting-ready-to-die me some mothaphucka's up in that hospital - space or whatever it was suppose to be.

Soon after my blowup, I overheard one of the nurses talking about it on the phone. I recognized the woman because she was the one who came in the room initially. And it was her that was so eager to tell me, "Mr. Humphrey informed us to do nothing other than make her comfortable."

"Mr. Humphrey! I don't give a fuck about what no Mr. Humphrey say. He don't run shit and what you calling him for?"

She got smart and replied, "Apparently he does sir. He is named as the executer of the estate and power of attorney, and he is the signature that's on her hospice information."

"So! What that mean? I'm her family. That nigga just a family friend, and he bout to not be that!"

"Well, sir, where you present for the hospice application that took place earlier today?"

"Yes, I was present, but I refused to be a part of it."

"Well, I'm sorry sir, but you may have forfeited your rights. We have to call Mr. Humphrey regarding any changes that are to be made giving that he is the only signature on Ms. Sanders' paperwork."

"Man, I don't need nary som' bitch permission to get no glass of water for my grandmother!"

I walked right across the hall into another hospice room where there was a lady sitting with her dying mother, I guess. I saw one of them hospital jugs in that hospice room and took it right in front of their face.

"Excuse me, but I'll bring this right back to ya' when I'm through."

I went back to my grandmother's room, emptied that somebody-else's-hospice-room water out and put some fresh Hydria water in that bad boy. I got a face towel, dipped and soaked it in it a time or two. Still being mindful of the stroke thing they were talking 'bout. I put it to her mouth and let her suck on the towel as I squeezed a little bit. Man she was *real* thirsty. She damn near sucked all the towel out that water. I even put some in a cup with a straw and let her suck it. It didn't seem like shit was wrong with her throat to me.

Then, she had the nerve to say she was hongry. Not hungry, but *hongry*.

Oh, no she didn't! I went on a Hell's Angels tour around that hospice center. Of course, they refused to give me anything for her to eat, so I went around to each room on that floor and proceeded to jack every piece of biscuit left a patient could eat in that hospice or anything that looked like my grandmother was able to consume without choking. With all the food I found we could have made a pantry.

Once I realized she could swallow some of that day-old hospice biscuit that somebody's relative had leftover to eat, I was willing to feed it to her everyday after that. And she was more than willing to eat it.

The entire hospice came down with food and water when they weren't supposed to. When it was done and she realized her boys were putting up a fight for her life, she decided she was gon' put up one too. I knew she did. She didn't say anything. She didn't have to once she released that big gate-mouf wide smile upon us...mm-mp! Nothing needed to be said.

That smile said, *"That's my boys! That's my boys!"*

Now what grandson wouldn't see the life in that? Didn't look nothing like "*dies*"to us, and Dorothy Sanders grandsons were 'bout to tear that hospice place up...inside out...for their grandmother. They had life messed up, but as I fed my grandmother the last bite of the biscuit I sat beside my brother looking and feeling victorious. We both felt the sentiments of our late great Uncle Bernie Mac, *"We ain't scared of you mothaphuckas!"*

CHAPTER 29

WE GON' FIGHT

Things got a little crazy at that hospice place last night, or this morning. Derrick was still aggravated about that key situation and this person who appeared to be a new visitor to me turned out to be one of our long lost aunts. She had been helping our grandmother out while me and Derrick were off doing God knows what to who and where.

Derrick was already familiar with her, but she was still a long lost auntie as far as I was concerned. I had never met her, let alone heard of her.

She was all chummy, hugging on me immediately when she arrived, staring at me and shit. I almost thought she was attracted to me because she was looking at me so hard and happy-like.

She kept repeating, "Ooh baby, you looking just like Button." Button was my daddy's nickname. The name my grandmother would be hallucinating to or with during her illness at times. People always were saying that I looked like my daddy. I never saw him alive, only pictures and not a one with he and I, or my brother together. I always wondered why? There was no denying the resemblance though, I was the splitting image of him.

At any rate, the first thing was "auntie's" name was Lula Bell.

Yeah, Lula Belle and she was about as country as her name, mouth and mind going a hundred miles an hour, in overtime.

I began to tell her how mama woke up eating and drinking last night. Hell, I was excited and couldn't wait for her to awake again to see if she had an appetite still. My grandmother was gon' be the first one to wake up and walk up out of a hospice is what I was thinking, but Lula Belle looked startled in the face and I couldn't figure out why.

Then she asked, "Did you sign the hospice papers baby?"

That question ruined our relationship before it got started good for me. I didn't want to talk to nobody who wanted to talk about no damn hospice. I wanted to talk about home for my grandmother, not hospice. Her and Derrick could discuss that shit. I wondered how she knew about the papers anyway? Then she brought up Humphrey.

"Had Humphrey discussed the insurance policy left in y'alls' name?"

That really got Derrick's attention being he wasn't allowed in the house to verify anything. So he started bitching about that key issue again, especially when Lula Belle said she just left the house and she had a key.

Her and my uncle saw Mama Dorothy's policy a few years earlier when one of their other cousins died and her policy wasn't in order. So they brought it to Mama Dorothy's attention just in case hers was not in order. At that time, she showed them where it would be in case of a situation. So while at the house last night, they proceeded to look for it again.

Well, my brother was really animated now. Hyperventilating damn near. He wanted to know why Lula had a key when Humphrey said nobody was allowed in the house due to the law of the will and all that shit.

Right after she confirmed Derrick's notions about Humphrey being a crook, she said, "Call him."

Initially, Derrick was rolling his eyes behind her back like she was messy, but now he and her had become best friends that quick, because they had some common interests. Humphrey, that house key, and now the insurance policy.

None of that shit was sinking in with me because I was still in denial about all of it.

"SHE AIN'T DYING, Y'ALL," I yelled out. "So why are we planning on it?"

They looked at me stunned and startled for a second or two... paused...and then continued back to talking to each other like, "*shiiit, nigga you in denial, we ain't. We getting prepared.*"

I simply let them trip about all of that. I kept looking at the clock 'cause mama had been sleeping a while.

"Humphrey is downstairs again," Derrick said. I began to notice that he and Humphrey stayed in communication with each other some kind of quiet.

They all started to look like some crooks to me and my mind began to replay some of that conversation between Derrick and Lula Belle when they went downstairs to meet Humphrey.

Go downstairs to meet him for what? Let that mothaphucka come upstairs. That also got me to thinking. Why was Lula Belle and her husband looking for that policy so much anyway? That was a lil' nosey to me. Hell, she hadn't even been to the hospital yet and she was in my grandmother's house looking for dead shit already, while my grandmother was still alive.

Fuck it, I thought. *That's them greedy mothaphuckas.* I was there for my grandmother, not what she had to leave us.

Some hours passed and the nurse came in preparing to put something in Mama Dorothy's IV.

"Excuse me, but what is that?" I asked.

"Morphine sir."

I immediately caught my snap! That was why she was sleeping so much.

"No! Don't give her no more," I said, jumping from my seat. "That's why she ain't waking up, and as long as y'all doping her up with that she ain't gon' wake up to eat. And as long as she can't eat, she can't survive." This had to be some type of conspiracy, or something.

In my mind, I tried to sell myself on the idea that this was hospice and mama was here to be comfortable. *Nope Eric, that's what hospice do...make them comfortable.* But the best of me would not accept it. *Comfortable for what though? Yeah, to die and we ain't tryin' to die up in hur...up in hur.*

"It's a bad decision not to give her pain medicine because she will be in too much pain, and we are here to make her comfortable."

Whatever, I thought.

"If you can feel pain, you alive is all I know, and that's all we're concerned with. DON'T GIVE HER ANOTHER SHOT!"

Once again, they claimed they was gon' call Humphrey, the hospice doctors and everything.

"Well, sir I will have to call her power of attorney, the doctors and my supervisor if you will not allow me to give your grandmother anything."

"I don't give a shit. Call him. He downstairs and I wish he would come up here and defend this shit in front of me. You gon' get all the Humphrey kicked out that mothaphucka man!"

Humphrey got wind of my attitude apparently. Because he never came into that room ever again while I was there. That slimy mothaphucka would come to the nurses' station only to check on the status of my grandmother. After that, he would only call.

I could care less because I didn't need to see his ass. I wasn't there for him anyway, but I bet ain't nobody doping her up no more until she wake up and say she ain't hungry or thirsty. *I mean that!*

Well, as I said, it got a little tense with Derrick, Lula Belle and Humphrey earlier. Humphrey took the key from Lula Belle and gave it to Derrick but asked him not to enter the premises until it was admissible through the courts, as in regards to Wills and Deaths in the state. I assumed Derrick agreed, but that didn't mean he was gon' comply. Not if he was anything like me, his older brother.

Surprisingly, it looked like he was gonna do just that. Otherwise, he would have been getting over there first chance he got. It probably was because neither he, nor Humphrey, trusted Lula Belle with a key since it was brought to their attention that she was over there probing.

Obviously, Lula Belle wasn't too happy anymore either. She never came back up to check on my grandmother and she was really beginning to smell fishy to me. That was okay, mama had me and Derrick there now, or did she? Well fuck it, I knew she had me.

We managed to make it through the night without incident. I was hoping Derrick made sure they didn't give her anymore morphine during the night and they must have not because by the time I got there that morning she was waking up. She was her usual witty self.

"There he is, Mr. Big or Big Shot himself," she said when she recognized me. She always made reference to my presence being commanding like my grandfather. ,She used to always say, "He could walk in The White House and command attention from the president." I never knew what she really meant. I thought she was teasing me or something for thinking I'm somebody when I wasn't ...yet.

Anyway, we shot the shit with each other a while. She was something crafty and witty, funny and stern at the same time. I just used to dream when I looked at her or talked to her. It wasn't like that with my other grandmother. I mean, I loved her too, but my daddy's mama she made me think or grow every time I was in her presence.

The day was going along just fine until one of the nurses came along and caught me feeding her. To me, I wasn't *caught* doing nothing, but I assumed that's what she thought it was...caught. Hell, she was my grandmother and it wasn't an accident that I was her grandson. And well, that feeding...that was by design too. I deliberately was doing that too. I didn't see the *caught* in none of that. Nevertheless, she proceeded to warn me about the consequences of feeding mama. I proceeded to act like she wasn't in that room talking to me. She got unheard and finally went on about her business.

We didn't have very many visitors that day. I guess, rumor got back to that usher board that Sister Sanders had drama going on behind her belongings.

Derrick returned in time enough for me to go to work. He and mama were up talking when I left. She was in good spirits and seemed to be improving by the hour. That was a good sign until the next day, when one of the nurses came in there trying to blow our high.

"They usually get better before they get worse," the skinny, long-faced nurse had the nerve to say. "They will only **appear** (as she put a strong emphasis on the appear part) to get better..."

I wanted to say, "Bitch, that may be the case for somebody else's grandmother, but this was "my" grandmother," putting emphasis on **my**.

But instead, I told her, "For *my* grandmother, this ain't no *appear*...reappear maybe. We getting better and that ain't no accident either. That too is by design."

She hurried up and got her natural born skinny long white-faced ass up out of there, I betcha that. However, the day was coming to an end and I did notice mama was sleeping a lil' longer.

It wasn't until I was getting ready to go to work again that a few of the ladies from the church arrived. I was ready to get out of there, when one of them said, "She always sleep when we come."

Then another one spoke up and said, "Oh, they put a lil' morphine patch on her too."

"MORPHINE! And a patch, what's that?" I asked her, losing my cool. When she showed it to me, it was a lil' circle Band-Aid on her neck. "No wonder she hadn't woke up to eat again. These mothaphuckas don' slicked me again. I told them no more morphine. She ain't gon' live if she don't eat!"

I was livid around that hospice. I was about to wake everybody in the hospice, got damn it. Aint nobody gon' sleep up in hur...up in hur.

And I ain't going to work. I was gon' watch these mothaphuckas like a hawk. Finally, all the nurses came down there trying to calm me down. They were trying to counsel me about the pain and agony she would be going through if they didn't give her the morphine.

"Mothaphucka! What part of pain don't you understand as it relates to being alive?! We wanna go through some alive pain. It's the *dead* pain we trying to avoid."

I was making so much noise it woke up mama. Apparently, she had been just'a listening without uttering a word.

Just then, I noticed my brother coming in and I was sure he heard me coming up the corridor because he burst in the room fearing something was wrong. I immediately pointed to the Band-Aid and explained to him what it was.

Everybody was pleading their case to us. From the church ladies to the doctors that arrived after the nurses summoned them to get some order in the room. I didn't want to hear from nobody but mama, so I turned to her as I went to one side of her bed with the church ladies and doctors at the foot.

I said, "Mama...you making us nervous."

She raised up one hand and grabbed my hand squeezing it. And lifted the opposite hand as my brother rushed to the other side to grab it.

"Mama...you wanna fight?" I spoke humble but sternly. We gonna fight as long as you gonna fight. Do you wanna fight?" I asked.

She squeezed my hand pulling herself up a bit as she pulled us in closer and looked us dead in the face with that big, gate-mouf wide smile and said, "Do you wanna fight?" grinning mischievously.

I said, "We fighting!"

"Well, let's fight then," she simply said and lowered herself back down flat onto the bed.

Get y'all ass outta here! Get the fuck up outta here is what I was feeling, but I didn't say it. Matter of fact, I didn't say another word to any of them. The law had spoken. So it was written and so it shall be done got damn it! My grandmother said _we fighting_. What they didn't know was that didn't mean just fighting if you were a Sanders. That meant kickin' ass! But not just in that hospice...if you had Sanders' blood that meant kickin' ass in life too.

I was beginning to sense and feel that responsibility. Beginning to feel the difference that this blood seem to always make. I was growing in her presence, again. I was becoming a man, and it was about time I started behaving like one. It was time to man up. It was time to fight.

CHAPTER 30

BLESS YOUR HEART

After my grandmother said she was ready to fight, I think we went and made a few groceries making rounds to each and every hospice room. Not really, but she had more than enough dried up biscuits to eat in that room and she was being fed and feeding herself for at least a day and a half. She didn't show any signs of pain, except maybe a grimace or two here and there.

As soon as me or my brother would say her name, "Mama! What you doing over there?" she would immediately replace that agony on her face with that big ole gate-mouf wide smile and that was fine by us. We understood she may have to go through some pain. I mean, it was gon' get worse before it got better right? But what could be better than living when everybody around seems to be pulling for you to die? That's how it seemed to be to me.

Humphrey, maybe he was tired of having to see after our grandmother. Lula Belle, maybe she was waiting on her pot of gold at the end of the rainbow. And maybe the church, some of them...come to think of it not the church...but Lula Belle's usher board committee, maybe they needed a funeral to go to or something fascinating to talk about. 'Cause it didn't appear any of them had a life. Somebody's funeral could have been some form of entertainment, especially one they would be performing at.

Well, it wasn't going to be any of that now. Mama said she wanted to fight and she had two of the most important people in the world alive and in her life, next to God, that she needed to fight with her. Her one and only dead son's offspring. In fact, she always held on to my dad's hand in spirit. Now, he was still holding onto hers and he left us behind to see after his mother, is how I looked at it.

The next couple of days were quiet and drawn out. We didn't have too many visitors 'cause mama was beginning to have a lot of pain. We thought it was part of the getting well process, so we stopped disturbing her or calling her name when she would get an attack of agony in some part of her body.

I took off work for a couple of days to keep an eye on her. Derrick and I never left her side. We made an agreement that if something happened to her we would *only* inform the other. We wanted to be the first to know of a change in her condition.

At night, she would be in so much pain. Her urine began to turn brown and she was losing her appetite. I was suddenly reminded of the nurse's sentiments a few days earlier when I was bitching. *They appear to get better before they get worse,* putting emphasis on "appear."

The doctors said we were really taking a chance at her last days being filled with pain if we denied the morphine and we might not forgive ourselves afterwards. They said her organs would begin to shut down and one way of telling would be that her urine would turn brown. It wouldn't be long after that.

I couldn't take my eyes off that urine bag hanging down beside the bed. I became a student in that room. My honing device in my belly would pick up on any changes. My radar wasn't gonna allow anything to float beneath it at this point. My extra sensory perception was at its highest, sensitive keen.

For two days and nights, I sat in the recliner only getting up to go to the bathroom. My brother sat on one side of the bed as I sat on the other. We kept the TV at a real low volume so we could hear her at all times. At times, she tried to fool us like she was okay by calling out our names. And we would answer, "I'm here Babygirl or what you over there fussin 'bout woman." Anything to create some normalcy. As usual, that great big gate-mouf wide smile would show up out of nowhere. I sensed she received great joy.

Even though we hadn't been around like maybe we were supposed to, she always knew we'd be there when it counted. I often thought about my mama. I couldn't even tell Mama Dorothy about her death, but I'd give anything to have been there for her when she was in the hospital in her final hour now...anything. However, I knew my mama would be proud of me being there for my dad's mama. Not just being there but being there for the right reasons. To save her life.

On the next morning, mama was in more pain than usual, but she was fighting and as long as she was fighting we was gon' stomach it. Neither me nor my brother showed any signs of wavering in our decision. We just watched her not saying a word to each other each time she would moan, but I could feel him, and I know he could feel me. We became one in that room, at that time. We had an objective and nothing else was important.

The pain seemed to be surmounting to the point of excruciating. We were torturing ourselves and I remember it crossing my mind that neither Humphrey, nor Lula Belle, had come back to the hospital. At that point, a knock on the door broke into my thoughts. It was three of the church ladies that weren't part of Lula Belle's crew. Mother Lou, Ruby Jean, and Faye – another lady I had a crush on my entire life besides Ms. Belinda. I was glad to see them and especially Faye. When they had come before, mama was sleep, but this time she was awake and in a grave amount of pain.

The reason we liked them was because they didn't treat her like she was sick. They cut up as they always did with her.

"Hey ole lady, Rev. say he looking for you at church Sunday," Mother Lou would say.

"Rev. say he can't trust nobody to count his money but you Dorothy" chimed Ruby Jean.

Faye took a brush to her salt and pepper mini fro to grandmother's delight while suggesting, "You and these boys giving these hospital people a time ain'tcha?" She was mindful enough to say hospital instead of hospice.

They really warmed up that room and we couldn't have been

more appreciative at that pivotal time.

Mama Dorothy was her typical witty self replying with something only she could come up with. For about fifteen minutes, it was like a lil' Baptist Comedy Family Reunion in there. But even they could see she was putting on face.

One of the nurses came in and lifted up her blanket to feel her feet, ankles and knees and mama let out a scream and jumped something terrible. The nurse immediately looked at me with a stern look and suggested, "Sir, we really should give your grandmother a shot of morphine to ease her pain. She is in a great amount of pain."

"NO!" I answered looking her square in the face because her sternness had nothing on mine...I was a Sanders. "It's just a lil' pain. If she can go through it, we can."

Mama tried to look like she wasn't in any or that much pain.

What I could appreciate about Mother Lou, Ruby Jean and Faye was they respected our decision whether they felt differently about it or not. They didn't butt in like the usher board church ladies did without asking any questions.

The nurse, however, left and I sat back down. Just as soon as I got back down in my seat good, she returned with two more doctors. After touching, poking and prodding all over mama, I imagine she would be in pain.

I got up and said, "Just leave her alone then. You poking all over her, of course she is gon' hurt."

They once again pleaded, "Mr. Payson, trust us..."

I didn't even let them complete a sentence. "Trust you! Man I don't know you. I trust this..." Ipointing at my gut.

They were so convinced in their attempts, they damn near started arguing with me. This went on about twenty minutes until I heard something in the background of all our bickering. It was faint like that whisper I heard when I was a little boy upon that bedroom window that night somebody was after my daddy... caught and killed him. We looked down and it was mama grimacing with that gate-wide smile at the same time.

She reached up for my hand, looked me dead in the eye, and whispered, "Let 'em give it to me baby...let 'em give me the shot.

Mama hurtin'."

I said, "You sure?"

I could see the agony in her eyes as she replied, "Yeah baby...it hurt too bad." She didn't shed a tear.

I looked at the doctor with defeat in my eyes and failure on my mind and guilt in my soul.

"Give her the shot."

They immediately began prepping needles for her IV. As I attempted to let her hand go and walk away, she grabbed it tighter, pulling me to her side, looked me in my eye and said, "Bless your heart baby...bless your heart." She patted the top of my hand with her other hand.

I kissed her on her mouth and I could feel the death seeping into her and into me at that moment. I couldn't hold it back. I burst into tears like the same lil' nine-year-old scared little boy that was afraid to take a bath by himself, because his daddy seemed to always be in the tub. My radar told me after that shot she would never wake up again.

Mother Lou, Ruby Jean and Faye were there to try to console me some. I couldn't get out the room fast enough before it belted out, falling to the ground. I desperately didn't want her to see me crying, but the guilt and pain was too overwhelming.

Bless your heart were the last words I ever heard my grandmother say and they're the words I hear most often when I think of her. I often wonder if she even really fully understood my devotion to her, even in my absence. Bless your heart confirmed that for me. Years I agonized over doing the right thing, but after seeing her in hospice I started to manifest into the man she always envisioned me being. I understood though that I may not have been around like a grandson should. I may not have had anything to offer to her and at times could have been an embarrassment.

That bless your heart meant, ***I now know you are gon' be alright and be everything I knew you could be.*** The fact that I was willing to fight for her life, fight for her death, fight for her right to fight until her very last breath...that made me right to her. That made it right, that made it alright.

Mama Dorothy died December 7, 2007 holding my hand,

massaging my heart, securing my soul...and I ain't never lettin' go.

New Tonesetter

Never Let Go of My Hand

By Kerry E. Wagner

Cost: $9.99
Not including Shipping &
Handling

Other Titles from The Wag Group

She Did That

Take an incredible mind blowing ride through 34 exhilarating chapters. This novel breaks down silent barriers men andwomen so often encounter with its brutal truths and catchy phrases that ring out loud "reality check!" To those playing the game, yet those willing to be exposed, this book serves us with SECRETS we can all learn from. Raw and uncut, **She Did That** raises your awareness and reminds you not to forget consequences and to remember responsibility in love. *"Climax in every chapter,"* says Mia Davis of Literary Minds Book Club Association. "You will laugh out loud, find yourselfenraged while crying immensely, and dare to ask yourself, *what does LOVE have to do with it?"* NOTHING...unless your life depends on it!

DEFINITE PAGE TURNER AND A TRUE LOVE STORY AT ITS FINEST! A MUST READ," SAYS THE CONVO CAFE" IN NEW YORK.

Stay tuned to the sequel to Never Let Go Of My Hand.

Bless Your Heart

WAG FEST

WagFest Litertainment is more than a literary conference and bazaar; it is a movement that promotes self sufficiency and resourcefulness. Although not exclusive, Wagfest caters to independent and self published authors, poets, musicians, comedians, and artist. Started in 2007 in New Jersey, a close knit group of authors got together in the spirit to sell books and have a good time. Since then, a second WagFest (Seattle) in March 2008 and third WagFest (Cincinnati) in October 2008 proved to be huge successes with a larger group of artists and fans traveling cross country to participate in this event. The saying at WagFest is "come as strangers but leave as family" and that has proven true time and time again.

Most artists know that building a successful career out of their art takes time, dedication, and support. Support is something that our families are sometimes not willing to give readily. In linking up with WagFest, you have a community that will back you and as we grow so do YOU!

Self-Published Authors and proud of it, so come out and share in the spirit of creativity, entertainment, and entrepreneurship. One thing about WagFest Litertainment, we don't have to claim to be the best because we are nothing like the rest!

Kerry E. Wagner is a native Houstonian. He is affiliated with various entertainers in the Houston area. After devoting years to Houston's underground rap scene, this former rapper took 18 years of experience and was compelled to change the game of urban literature. He was first inspired to publish his work after reading New York Bestseller, "Coldest Winter Ever," by Sister Souljah.

Kerry began writing his first novel after being incarcerated. Without the means to seek a publisher, Kerry E. Wagner lived and wrote the fictional masterpiece "She Did That" while living out of his car. He went to the library everyday and took notes free hand because he was computer illiterate at the time.

Initially, his manuscript was over 800 handwritten pages, a testament to his hard work, perseverance, and drive. Kerry created an audio version of the first three chapters of "She Did That" to test market in area beauty salons and on local college campuses. This strategy created a roaring demand and he was able to build a grand following on the underground circuit. He made frequent appearances on the message boards and forums of Michael Baisden, Russ Parr, Reggie Johnson and Steve Harvey, becoming very popular in online communities.

To Schedule Speaking Engagements or Guest Appearances for
Kerry E. Wagner,
Contact: Assuanta Collins, Personal Publicist
E-mail:acollins@astaprservices.com
Tele: 678-833-9130

Visit web site: www.astaprservices.com.